A
POCKET FULL
OF POSIES

SHAWN SARLES

SCHOLASTIC

Copyright © 2022 by Shawn Sarles

All rights reserved. Published by Scholastic Inc., *Publishers since 1920*. SCHOLASTIC and associated logos are trademarks and/or registered trademarks of Scholastic Inc.

The publisher does not have any control over and does not assume any responsibility for author or third-party websites or their content.

No part of this publication may be reproduced, stored in a retrieval system, or transmitted in any form or by any means, electronic, mechanical, photocopying, recording, or otherwise, without written permission of the publisher. For information regarding permission, write to Scholastic Inc., Attention: Permissions Department, 557 Broadway, New York, NY 10012.

This book is a work of fiction. Names, characters, places, and incidents are either the product of the author's imagination or are used fictitiously, and any resemblance to actual persons, living or dead, business establishments, events, or locales is entirely coincidental.

ISBN 978-1-338-79401-4

10 9 8 7 6 5 4 3 2   22 23 24 25 26

Printed in the U.S.A.   40

First edition, September 2022

Book design by Christopher Stengel

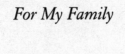

For My Family

CHAPTER
ONE

Parker ducked her head as she darted through the dark neighborhood streets, the slap of her feet carrying her through the empty night.

Don't look back.

She rounded the corner, her heart thundering in her throat, her breath catching in her chest.

Don't slow down.

Tears pricked at the inside corners of her eyes, threatening to spill down her cheeks.

Don't think about Dani.

This thought, however, was the one that tripped her up. A stitch dug into her side. She stumbled and threw out a hand, bracing herself as she fell against a brick wall. The grit coated her palm, sandpaper rubbing her raw, opening her up. Her heaving breaths echoed off the building, ricocheting right back into her ears.

It wasn't her fault.

They'd both known the risks.

Dani would be fine.

But no matter how many times Parker told herself this, she couldn't shake the doubt. The guilt. She couldn't forget what she'd done.

Fingers shaking, she reached into her pocket and pulled out her phone. She stared at the empty screen, waiting for Dani to tell her she was okay. That she'd gotten out, too. They couldn't lose everything over a stupid prank.

But they hadn't had a choice. They were freshmen. How could they possible skirt around initiation? They were instructed to break into their rivals' school and take pictures with the district championship trophy. Then, before leaving, they would have to cut the strings on every one of their rackets, a parting gift so the girls would know they'd been there.

Dani hadn't wanted to do it. She and Parker had argued about it earlier that day. Breaking into another school and taking a picture was one thing. But destroying those rackets crossed the line. It was property damage. And what if they got caught? They could get kicked off the team. They could lose their scholarships. Was it really worth the risk?

But these girls were rich, Parker had argued. They could afford new strings. And going through with the prank was the only way they were ever going to fit in at their new school. On their new team. The other girls didn't care how good they were on the court. This was the only way to earn their respect and make things better.

Dani still hadn't wanted to go through with it, but Parker had insisted. She needed this, and she'd used her best-friend pull to convince Dani that she needed it, too.

So they did it. They broke into the school. They got their snapshot with the trophy. But then, with the twang of that first snipped string still vibrating in the air, a walkie-talkie crackled. A flashlight swept through the room. A security guard burst through the door and started shouting for both of them to remain still and put their hands where he could see them. And without thinking, Parker had done something stupid.

She'd jumped up, rushing toward the man. She'd knocked into him before he knew what was happening, booking it right through the open door and into the hallway, where she didn't hesitate—not for a second.

As she'd bolted away, she'd ignored the guard's cries for her to stop. She'd only thought about her own freedom. She'd left Dani behind to take the fall. She'd abandoned her best friend. And now she had no idea what would happen to her.

Dani would get suspended. Maybe even be put on probation. And what if she lost her scholarship? What if she got kicked off the team? Parker couldn't play tennis without her. They were doubles partners. They were supposed to have each other's backs.

Parker slowed her pace once she felt certain that no one had followed her. She wanted to scream. She wanted to go back in time and change what she'd done, but she couldn't. And the worst part was that even though she was furious at herself, a part of her felt relieved that she'd gotten away.

Her parents were dealing with enough as it was. They couldn't even make it through dinner without dropping into an uncomfortable silence, the kind where Parker focused on the food on her plate to avoid all the things her parents wouldn't say in front of her.

But she still heard their whisper fights at night, still saw the frustrated looks her mom leveled at her dad every time he sat down in his recliner or disappeared into the bedroom for a nap. Parker couldn't help but notice the way her mother hesitated at the grocery store, taking a few items out of their cart before they checked out.

Her mom had reached the end of her patience, and Parker worried about what would happen next. The last thing her parents needed was her getting into trouble at school. Or worse, getting expelled. Something like that could set off an explosion and blow her family apart for good.

Parker slapped her phone against her thigh as she took a deep breath, leaning against the gritty wall for support. She glanced around, but the streets were still deserted. She was still alone. Guilt squeezed her insides, wringing her out until her heart hiccuped. She smacked her leg again, happy when it stung. And then again. She didn't know if Dani would forgive her. She didn't know if she should. What if Dani got expelled? She and Parker weren't rich kids like the rest of them. Scholarship kids didn't get second chances.

Suddenly, Parker's phone came to life in her hand. She whipped it around, but it wasn't Dani.

It was Callie, their team captain, checking in on them. Had they finished the prank? Did they get the photographic proof? Parker didn't know what to say. She still couldn't think straight. So she came out with the truth, let it spill from her fingertips before hitting send.

Three dots appeared on her screen while Callie typed and Parker could only hold her breath. Could only wait and pray for a miracle—that Callie might have some way out of this.

You got caught?

The message popped up, and Parker heard her captain's anger in those three words.

How stupid are you?

Did Dani tell on us?

Is she going to rat us out?

You're going to get us all in trouble.

5

Teammates don't snitch on each other.

Does Dani know that?

Are you going to remind her?

Have you thought about where your loyalties lie?

You better make the right choice.

You don't want to be BB forever, do you?

Parker froze as she read the last text from Callie. She flinched at the nickname, Callie making her threat clear.

Not that it was a surprise. That was the only currency their captain seemed to understand. Why had it taken Parker so long to realize that? Why hadn't she stood up to the senior? Or at least questioned her leadership? Her rules? These initiation stunts she'd forced them to pull?

But Parker knew why. It was because Parker needed a reset from that horrifically embarrassing first day. She needed to get rid of that nickname. Of *BB*. She wanted to have friends. She wanted the rest of the team to like her.

But she didn't care about any of that now.

"Where are you, Dani?"

Parker's whisper came out as a prayer. One that, after a

couple of minutes, hadn't been answered. So, pocketing her phone, she turned and kept walking, making her way through the streets on autopilot, her mind wrapped up in everything else. She didn't even realize she'd made it to her apartment building and up the four flights of stairs until her keys jingled as she pulled them out.

Parker stopped, recognizing it was past her curfew. Pressing her ear to the door, she listened hard for signs of life. Would her parents be fighting? Had they even realized she'd snuck out?

In the past couple of months, Parker had pretty much been able to do her own thing. Her parents had been so consumed by their own troubles that they'd left her alone. She knew they wouldn't have checked on her in her room. Which meant she had to be quiet. If she could sneak in, then she wouldn't get into any more trouble.

Holding her breath, Parker slowly inserted the key into the lock. She twisted the knob a fraction at a time, wincing as the latch popped free, a sliver of light peeking out from the apartment. She inched the door open just enough to squeeze inside and took the same amount of care closing it behind her. Then she paused, standing there on her own welcome mat, waiting to see if her parents would barge in and catch her.

But no one appeared. No one seemed to have heard her late arrival. This might have been the first lucky turn of the night.

Rising to her tiptoes, Parker crept down the hallway. She snuck through the empty kitchen and slunk past the living room, where the TV was on even though no one seemed to be in there watching it. She got to her bedroom and could just make out the sound of muffled voices, the light seeping out from underneath her parents' door, blinking as they paced back and forth on the other side. Parker slid into her room. She didn't dare risk listening in on them. It could only be bad.

Safely inside her room, Parker tore off her jacket. As she threw it on the floor, the night began to catch up to her. Her head started spinning. Her mind began racing again. Her stomach flipped until she thought she might throw up. She grappled to slow down, to regain some kind of steadiness. But then she saw the photo on her dresser. Dani's face staring back at her, a trophy hoisted between their interwoven arms.

Parker gulped, feeling the lump work its way down her throat. She remembered that day when she and Dani had won their first tournament. City champions in their age group. How could Parker face her now? How would Dani ever be able to trust her on the court again?

Parker had left her in that equipment room to take full responsibility for a prank that Dani hadn't even wanted to do in the first place. And at the end, Parker hadn't even turned around when her best friend had whisper-screamed her name. Parker hadn't slowed down at all, too focused on saving her own skin.

But Parker heard it now. She remembered the moment. The betrayal in Dani's voice. How her whisper had deflated at the end, falling with the realization that Parker wasn't coming back for her.

Parker jumped as her phone vibrated with an incoming call. She peeked at it, knowing exactly who it'd be but dreading it all the same.

She wasn't ready. She hit the decline button, quickly cutting her phone off again when another call came through right after.

What could she say? She didn't know how to apologize. Her words wouldn't be enough. They couldn't rewind the clock.

What happened to you?

Where'd you go?

Parker?

How could you leave me there?

The messages came through fast, lighting up Parker's phone in a long string.

Why are you ignoring me?

I know you're there.

Do you even care that I'm in SO much trouble?

They called the cops! And my parents!

They said I was breaking and entering.

Destroying personal property.

They said they could press charges.

Parker didn't want to read it, but she couldn't stop herself either. A panicky feeling was building in her chest, swelling like a balloon, pressing her lungs out, stretching her rib cage until she thought it might crack in two.

Hello? Are you going to respond?

You're supposed to be my best friend.

How could you leave me like that?

Say something.

Quit ignoring me!

The messages stopped suddenly, but that didn't make the

tight feeling in Parker's chest go away. Her whole body shook as she waited for more. She knew Dani. Knew that she wasn't done. She wouldn't let Parker off so easily. She never forgot someone who crossed her. And she never forgave them.

You can let Callie know that I didn't tell on anyone.

I know how to be a good teammate.

I know what loyalty means.

No. That wasn't fair. That was completely wrong.

Maybe you can convince Callie to be your partner when they kick me off the team.

Traitor.

A shiver ran through Parker as she read the last message. It was what she'd feared. Exactly what she'd expected. But she couldn't lose Dani. She couldn't give up on what felt like her only friend. Her *best* friend. She began tapping out a message, starting and deleting it over and over again. But before she could finish the text—before she could send anything—her bedroom door burst open.

Parker dropped her phone, shaking her hand out like she'd

burned it. Fear seized her whole body as she looked up at her mom, who'd just come barging in.

This was it. Dani's mom must have called and told her everything that had gone down. The prank and sneaking out. Getting caught. Parker pulled back, preparing for the worst—but was that a smile on her mom's lips?

Parker rubbed her eyes, baffled by what she saw. Her mom looked happier than Parker had seen her in months. She seemed elated, like she'd just won a free day at the spa or something.

"Is everything okay?" Parker asked, confused and still a little worried. Had her mother finally snapped?

"Your dad got a job!" Parker's mom shouted, the words flying out of her mouth like a battle cry. "A company wants him to overhaul their whole security system. Install cameras and silent alarms and everything."

"That's great," Parker managed to get out, thrown by the announcement. She didn't know why her mom had felt the need to tell her right then. Couldn't the good news have waited until the morning?

"And I know it's short notice . . . but they want us to move."

The smile had disappeared from her mother's face.

Parker suddenly felt dizzy. Dani's texts felt like they were still burning a hole in her chest while her mother's words echoed in her head.

"But they have a house already set up for us," her mother

said. "And it sounds like the cutest little town. It's got real charm. A good school and lots of gardens. The town's been around forever. It's one of the oldest settlements in America."

Her mother sounded like she'd memorized the welcome brochure.

"I know it's a lot. And it's sudden," her mother continued, looking at her anxiously, her brow furrowed, more words spilling out of her mouth. "But this could change everything for us. And we can take some time. Your dad can head up and start while we tie everything up here. It's just—he's been out of work for so long and we really need this."

Parker knew her mom was waiting on her. Knew that she had to say something. But it was all so sudden. It was all so big.

To buy some time, Parker bent over, her head spinning as she retrieved her phone.

They were moving?

Parker had spent her whole life here. She didn't know if she could pack up and leave. She didn't know if she could start over someplace new. What would she do without Dani?

Glancing down at her phone, Parker went numb. Dani had texted her again. And it wasn't good.

You know what?

You can keep whatever apology you're cooking up.

13

> It's too late.

> I'm done with you.

Parker couldn't breathe. She was trying to, but her lungs wouldn't work. Her throat had clogged up. She was going to pass out. Or vomit. Her vision went hazy as she stared at the screen, taking in Dani's last message.

She couldn't mean it. Dani couldn't be done with her. They'd been friends for half their lives. Besties. Dani couldn't be serious. She couldn't be ending—

"Is everything all right?"

Her mom's question came to her from far away.

"I know it's all happening so quickly. But we don't have to—"

"When?"

Parker's mom startled at the sudden question.

"When does Dad need to move?" Parker clarified.

"Next week," Parker's mom replied slowly, looking at her like she'd spoken in a foreign language.

"I want to go with him."

Parker surprised herself with the proclamation.

"I want to move now. All of us together."

"But what about school? What about your friends? What about Dani—"

"Please?" Parker cringed at the desperation in her voice,

at the way her bottom lip quivered. Her fingers clutched the hard case of her phone and she tried to hold back her tears.

"Well, if that's what you really want," her mom began, uncertain.

"It is," Parker jumped in. "I promise. A new start will be good for all of us."

Then, realizing she hadn't even thought to ask. "Where is it?"

CHAPTER
TWO

Two days.

That was all it had taken to uproot their entire lives and move from Washington, DC, across six states. Forty-eight hours and everything had changed.

On the drive up, Parker had watched her familiar, crowded city give way to rolling pastures and then a monotonous mass of suburban sprawl that she'd mostly slept through. But when her dad had nudged her awake several hours later, saying that they were close, she'd had to pinch herself.

Because this couldn't be real. Her family didn't belong in a place like this, in a picturesque little town tucked away on the southern tip of Massachusetts. In a place called Coronation.

But that was what the sign had read when they'd crossed into town. And Parker could believe it was a place where kings and queens lived. She could see the ocean crashing just outside her window. And on the other side, everything ahead of her was so green and spread out and perfect-looking. There weren't any apartment buildings in sight, just huge house after huge house, every single one with a neat garden out front. And as her dad turned into the driveway of one of the monstrosities, it hit her that this one was theirs. Their own house. Their own garden. It felt impossible. From the looks on her parents' faces, she could tell they felt the same way.

As Parker slammed the car door, she stretched her arms high over her head, rubbing her eyes as if she'd woken from a long, restless sleep. This was her new reality. The past weekend had been a whirlwind of packing and labeling and cleaning. Of saying goodbye—though there was one person Parker couldn't bear to face.

Glancing down at her phone now, she was relieved to see that she didn't have any messages waiting for her. Dani had made good on her promise. She was done with Parker. She hadn't texted her or commented on her moving day post. Parker knew it was what she deserved. But she couldn't get it out of her head. Would Dani notice her missing at school the next day? Would she wonder where she'd gone? Or would she move on like they'd never known each other at all?

Parker's grip tightened, and she stared harder at her phone. But when nothing changed, she reminded herself that this was for the best. She had no clue what she'd say if Dani did reach out. She just wanted to forget all about that night. About how she'd failed at being a best friend.

"What do you want?" her mom asked, and Parker blinked, coming out of her thoughts. "Your dad's grabbing dinner."

"Whatever," Parker mumbled, taking one last glance at her phone before putting it away.

"I'll be right back," Parker's dad said, bounding toward the car before setting foot inside their new home.

Maybe he was nervous to start his new job, knowing that so much was riding on it going well. Or maybe Coronation's grandeur was making him feel uncomfortable, too. Or maybe he was just tired from a day of driving.

As Parker watched him pull out into the street, she tried not to worry about it. There wasn't anything they could do about it now. They'd moved. They were citizens of Coronation. They just had to get used to it. There was no going back.

"I know it's hard to leave everything behind," Parker's mom said, sidling up next to her in the driveway. "But this place is going to be good for us. I can feel it."

Parker nodded, watching the car until it turned and disappeared. She hoped that was true. And judging by the grin on her mom's lips—the one that Parker hadn't seen in a very long time—she had a good feeling that it might be.

"Welcome home," her mom breathed excitedly, and Parker couldn't help but feel that contagious glee creeping over to her. She gave her mom a side hug and the two spun around together, facing their new house, the enormousness of it rising up right there in front of them.

"This is all ours?" Parker's eyes bulged as she took in the two-story behemoth.

It was unlike anything in their old neighborhood. The grass was freshly cut and the house's walls glistened in the April sun, as if a fresh coat of paint had been applied that morning. A giant veranda wrapped around the front, with a porch swing hanging cozily in one corner. And just beneath all of that, a waist-high, manicured hedge framed the perfect picture above it.

It was enormous. And way more space than they needed. It was the kind of place she imagined her old classmates lived in. Which made Parker wonder what they'd think of her now.

Those kids had always looked down on her. They'd seen her as a scholarship student, there because of a handout. They'd never invited Parker in. Never given her a chance. They'd gone out of their way to make her feel like an outsider. But things would be different here. At least, she hoped.

Taking in a deep breath, Parker tried to ignore those worries. She inhaled again and noticed the hint of something sweet in the air. Curious, she took a few steps forward and spied tiny flecks of red running through the hedges. She got closer, and then she finally realized what they were.

Roses.

Their buds were plump and green, just waiting to burst

forth with bright red blossoms. They quivered on their stems, dancing in the afternoon's light breeze, the sun shooting through their leaves and spotlighting the beauty to come.

Parker couldn't help herself. She reached forward and cupped a bud in one hand, being careful to avoid the thorns. She leaned in and put her nose right up to the tiny opening, where she could just see the spirals of the rose's red petals beginning to unfurl. She inhaled again and let that sweet scent fill her lungs, carrying her away.

"Isn't it divine?" a voice said.

Parker jumped and her hand slipped, snagging on a thorn. She felt a bright stab of pain and was shocked to see a drop of her own blood bubbling up on her finger. Without thinking, she stuck it in her mouth, the blood warm on her tongue, tasting of salt and sugar, the tang of iron reminding her of soil.

Parker turned and spotted a woman standing in the driveway next to her mother. The woman's blond hair was slicked back into a neat wave, and her tailored blouse and dress pants were ironed to perfection.

"Wait until everything starts blooming," the woman went on in a low tone, her voice confident and crisp, possessing the New England accent of someone who had lived here her entire life. "The scent fills the whole town, and there's nothing you can do to get away from it."

Parker yanked her finger out of her mouth as the woman started laughing a little too loudly at her own joke.

"I just wanted to pop over and welcome you all to the neighborhood," she said.

"That's very nice of you," Parker's mom said, sounding a bit flustered. And Parker understood why. She felt uncomfortable herself, in her rumpled sweatpants and road-worn T-shirt, standing in front of this impeccably dressed woman who looked like she'd walked out of a magazine. Parker couldn't take her eyes off the woman's rose-red lips as she opened them to introduce herself.

"I'm Rosalynn York from just down the street."

The woman tilted her head back, and Parker could see her pointing at the biggest house she'd seen yet.

The name seemed to have triggered something in Parker's mom as she took a quick step forward and offered a hand to the woman.

"York? As in the York Rosarium?"

"That's right. Family owned for almost two centuries."

The way the woman said it, with such pride, made Parker wonder what it felt like to have that kind of legacy.

"My husband and I—" Parker's mother stammered. "We're just so appreciative for the opportunity—for the job and everything—"

She motioned up toward the house, and it finally clicked. This was her dad's new boss. This was the woman who had hired him. Who'd brought them here.

"It's nothing." Mrs. York waved away the gratitude. "We're

excited to have your husband on board. I know he's going to be a valuable member of our team. And you all will be just as important to our little community, too, I hope."

"Well, we really are thankful," Parker's mom said as she tipped her head forward, bowing slightly. She gave Parker a sharp look out of the corner of her eye, and Parker immediately jumped in with her own thanks, though Mrs. York seemed completely uninterested as she glanced over her shoulder.

"Here he is."

The woman gestured grandly as a boy about Parker's age rounded the corner, his hair swooping perfectly back, their resemblance undeniable.

"My son, Brady."

The boy opened his mouth and two rows of bright-white teeth beamed at Parker and her mom.

"And a little housewarming gift for you all." Mrs. York took a plate of cupcakes from her son and handed them over to Parker. "I hope you like rose water."

Parker peered down at the treats, a rosette painstakingly piped on top of each one in red and pink icing.

"I'm sure they'll be delicious," Parker said, though she'd never had anything so fancy. Judging by the smell, though, she imagined they'd taste a little like soap. But she didn't want to insult their welcome committee. She didn't want to get her dad into trouble with his boss before he'd even started.

"Thank you."

Parker wondered if she should take a bite now or wait until later. She didn't know what the polite thing to do was. But she really didn't want to eat in front of Brady. She didn't want to have icing and crumbs all over her face. Even though he hadn't spoken a word yet, he was too cute for that to be his first impression of her. Luckily, Parker was saved from having to make a decision as Mrs. York plowed right on.

"You let me know if you need anything. Coronation is a small town, and we look out for each other."

"Well, I do have one question," Parker's mom mumbled, raising her hand slightly as if she needed to be called on. "I don't really have a green thumb. I mean, I can't even keep a houseplant alive for more than a few weeks." She laughed nervously, and Parker could see the embarrassment in the way her mom's shoulders pinched together. "I just don't want to be the reason those pretty flowers die."

Parker's mom blushed and pointed over to the hedges running along their new porch.

"Oh, don't worry about those." Mrs. York shooed Parker's mom's doubts away. "We have people who'll take care of the roses. They'll be around a few times a week to water and trim them. Don't pay them any attention. They won't bother you at all."

Parker's mom sighed and her shoulders loosened.

"Well, we'll let you all get settled now," Mrs. York said,

waving an effortless farewell. "Remember, we're here if you need anything. Oh, and before I forget. If it's alright, Parker, Brady is going to show you around school tomorrow."

Brady offered that megawatt smile of his. "More than happy to. Meet me out front of school in the morning."

Parker's heart skipped as the boy spoke for the first time. It surprised her that he didn't seem annoyed at his mom for volunteering his services. She knew his type. She knew that a boy like Brady—tall and cool and popular—wouldn't want to waste his time showing a little freshman like her around.

Thanking them one last time for the welcome cupcakes, Parker and her mom stood in the driveway and watched the Yorks walk away.

"They seem nice," Parker's mom concluded. "And Brady was cute."

"Mom." Parker flushed, because she had noticed how attractive he was, even if he was way out of her league. He looked like he'd fit right in at her old school. He wasn't the type of boy who would ever be interested in Parker.

"Let's check out the rest of the house," Parker's mom said. "And we can pick out your room."

Parker marveled at the thought of that. Would she even have enough stuff to fill her new space? Would she have one of those window seats she could nap on? Would she have an *actual* walk-in closet?

The possibilities buoyed Parker as she followed her mom

toward the house. But as she made her way up the front steps, she felt a sudden prick in her finger.

Looking down, she spotted where the thorn had left its mark. The tip of her finger had turned bright red, the cut not yet clotted. Parker lifted it to her mouth and sucked on the wound again, the iron tang stronger than before.

The scent of the roses came back to her suddenly, sweet and thick in her throat. Overpowering. She glanced down at the bushes and felt as though, impossibly, the buds were smiling at her. Dancing to a song only they could hear.

CHAPTER
THREE

Parker stood on the front steps of Coronation Country Day School, fidgeting in her uniform—the knee-length skirt, stiff white button-down, and navy sweater that had been hanging in her closet, waiting for her, at the new house. It was another gift, apparently, from Mrs. York, whose kindness was starting to creep Parker out. It wasn't normal. But then, at least Parker wouldn't stick out on her first day. Her mom hadn't had time to go shopping, so she didn't have anything to wear. Maybe this time she'd have a chance at fitting in.

But Brady was late, and she'd already awkwardly held the door open for five people. She didn't know what to do. She felt like an idiot for waiting. For being stood up. But hadn't she expected it of him? Hadn't she pegged him to be just like her old classmates? She should have listened to her gut. But it wasn't like she could ditch him now. She didn't know her way around, and she didn't want to seem ungrateful, not after his mom's grand welcome

Parker smoothed her skirt and patted down the collar of her shirt. She ran her fingers across her soft sweater, pausing as she brushed over the embroidered emblem hovering right against her heart, the pink threads tying themselves into a delicate rose. Her stomach tugged with a familiar queasiness as doubt crept in.

Could she do this? Could she survive on her own—without Dani?

Suddenly, Parker realized how much she missed her best friend. Her fingers itched to text her. She could use a pep talk. Dani had been good at that. She'd always had the right words to lift Parker's spirits, to get her pumped to take on anything. She'd always stood by Parker's side, even when Parker had humiliated herself on the first day of school last fall.

Parker's stomach rolled, her breakfast threatening mutiny. Before she could stop it, a memory pressed in and she saw herself over six months ago, that anxious freshman pacing the halls of a brand-new school in her secondhand uniform. The new girl. An outsider. She'd only gotten into the private academy because of a scholarship. She and Dani had won the under-fifteen DC city championships that summer and impressed the right people. But that didn't mean she belonged there.

A flush crept up Parker's neck as she remembered how flustered she'd been that day. She couldn't get her locker open, no matter how many times she tried. The combination just wouldn't work. And she could feel everyone swirling around her, talking loudly, their conversations flying behind her and over her and through her.

She just wanted to drop her bag and head to class. To find Dani, her one friend in all this chaos. But her locker wouldn't cooperate. And with each failed attempt, she grew more frustrated. More desperate. Until finally—she lost it. Her fist banged against the metal and she shouted like she'd just dumped an easy volley into the net.

Which had gotten everyone's attention.

Where she'd been invisible before, the whole hallway turned to look. All those eyes on her. Whispering. Laughing. Their phones out to record what the weird new girl would do next.

Parker had freaked. She'd broken away, abandoning her locker altogether. But the whispers had followed her, running down the hall, spreading like wildfire as fingers pointed in her direction. She didn't feel right. Her face was burning up and her stomach was rumbling. She gagged, and a vinegar tang washed over her tongue. She picked up her pace, searching for a bathroom. But she didn't know where it was, and she didn't have time to find it. And suddenly, it was too late.

She heaved and her breakfast came scorching up her throat, spewing out of her mouth with a retching noise that stopped every single conversation in the hallway.

Luckily, she'd managed to tear her backpack off at the last second and caught the vile concoction of oatmeal, orange juice, and stomach acid before it hit the floor. Before it splashed up and ruined someone's perfectly new loafers.

But everyone had seen. They were all jumping up and down, shouting to their friends, fake puking and then breaking out into laughter.

Hot tears filled Parker's eyes, and she sank to her knees, her backpack between her legs, full and warm to the touch. Dani had appeared out of nowhere then, rushing in and grabbing Parker by the shoulders, lifting her off the ground and pushing them both through the crowd that had formed.

They'd found a bathroom and she'd cleaned Parker up, wiping the spittle from her chin and convincing her that she could go back out there and face everyone. That it wasn't as bad as she thought.

But it had been. Parker's reputation had been cemented that morning, her nickname stamped across her forehead.

Barf Bag. *BB* for short.

The name had trailed her through the halls, making sure that no one wanted to sit with her at lunch or partner with her for lab. No one was willing to touch her. No one wanted to be her friend. No one except Dani.

Which was why Parker had wanted to do that tennis team prank so badly. Didn't Dani understand that? The risk of getting caught had been worth it. She needed the do-over. She needed to make a new name for herself.

Which was what she'd gotten, right?

The move to Coronation. The brand-new school. A do-over for the last two months of her freshman year. She didn't have Dani anymore, but that didn't mean she couldn't do this.

"Are you lost?"

Parker jumped at the sudden question and spun around. She started to open the door, but the girl who'd appeared at her elbow didn't make a move to go inside. Instead, she stood there, lips pursed, finger tapping her chin as she studied Parker, looking at her like she'd discovered some strange new creature.

"I don't recognize you," she finally stated, tilting her head to the side and brushing one of her long, silky braids over her shoulder.

"It's my first day," Parker mumbled, kicking herself when the statement came out as a question. She could do better than that. She needed to if she wanted things to be any different here.

"I'm waiting for Brady, actually. Brady York. He's supposed to give me a tour."

Parker sucked in her cheeks, wondering what this girl would do next. Was she about to get some awful new nickname? And all before she'd even walked through the school doors?

"You're going to be waiting awhile," the girl eventually said. "My brother's not exactly a morning person."

She smiled then, her teeth bright and white and straight.

Just as perfect as Brady's. And Parker saw the family resemblance, the girl's confidence and grace. An assurance that only came with popularity. And money.

"So you're a York, too?"

The girl nodded in a quick, excited motion.

"Which means you must be Parker."

Parker tried to match the girl's brilliant smile, but she couldn't keep the unease from souring her expression. This girl reminded her so much of Callie.

"Well, since my brother is tragically delayed, why don't *I* show you around?"

The idea popped out of the girl's mouth as if she'd plucked it right out of the sky.

"Oh." Parker tried to disguise her surprise. "No. I can't. I really should wait for him."

"We'll find Brady later," the girl assured Parker. And without any more delay, she looped her arm in Parker's and pulled her into the school.

"By the way, my name's Beth. I'll keep it to the highlights, but stop me if I'm going too fast."

Parker nodded before letting the girl whisk her away. She followed along as Beth took her past the auditorium and gymnasium, as she talked about the lunch schedule and where the best tables were situated, as she pointed out the teachers to avoid and the ones who didn't check homework assignments too carefully.

It was a lot to take in, but Beth somehow made it fun. What was the catch? When would this Callie lookalike start making her life hell? But before Parker knew it, they were back in the main lobby, their tour complete.

"So that's basically it," Beth proclaimed. "Everything you need to know. Do you have any questions?"

Beth twirled around and faced Parker. More students had trickled in by then and the hallways were getting crowded. But no one seemed to notice Parker's newness.

Parker shrugged. Beth had been pretty thorough.

"Not a single one?" Beth sounded disappointed.

"Uhm." Parker stalled as she tried to think, casting her eyes around the lobby, searching for something. "Who's that?" Parker pointed over Beth's shoulder, picking out a large portrait of a woman that was hanging against the wall. It was done in oils and looked really old and important. "She's kind of been all over."

And it was true. Parker had spotted her in just about every hallway and classroom, rendered in small and large portraits—and even in stained glass. She was unmistakable with the crown of roses perched in her long blond hair.

"Is she some kind of saint?" Parker went on. She didn't remember her mom telling her that this was a Catholic school, but she knew a lot of private schools were affiliated with a church. Her old school had been.

"That's Rosamund," Beth answered, nodding. She fell silent

as she stared up at the painting with a reverence that made Parker a little uncomfortable.

"Why's she so important?" Parker whispered, dropping her voice to meet Beth's sudden seriousness.

"She helped the original settlers of Coronation survive their first winter. She was an answer to their prayers."

Parker squinted as she tried to get a better look at the picture.

"At least, that's the story they tell," Beth went on, snapping out of her momentary daze. "Now she's just a reminder for us. A symbol to not give up hope. Tend to our gardens so that we might reap the benefits of what we sow." She added the last part with finger quotes.

A beat passed between them, Parker not knowing how to reply.

"I know. It's silly," Beth giggled as she waved it all away. "But it's nice to have the tradition. It brings us all together. And reminds us of where we came from. The town throws a spring festival in Rosamund's honor every year. It's kind of fun, actually. They say it helps with the harvest."

"Okay," Parker decided, even though it still seemed a bit odd to her.

"Now," Beth said, turning before Parker could ask any more questions. "Let's see if we can find my brother before morning chapel begins. He owes you an apology."

CHAPTER
FOUR

Organ music wafted through the air as Parker slid into the wooden pew, taking a seat next to Beth. They hadn't found Brady before the bell had rung, but Parker spotted him across the aisle now, his tie crooked and his hair still damp from the shower. He looked in his element, with his foot propped up on a pew, a group of boys sprawled around him, listening intently to whatever story he had to tell. He didn't seem guilty at all for no-showing on Parker—which meant that he was exactly the kind of guy Parker had assumed he'd be.

Sure, he'd been polite in front of his mom, bringing over those cupcakes and acting all nice and smiley. But then he'd turned around and completely ghosted her. Whatever. She could forget about him just as easily as he'd forgotten about her.

"My brother can be a bit of a jerk," Beth said, drawing Parker's attention away from Brady.

"It's fine," Parker mumbled, trying her best to look like she didn't care. "So do you all do this every morning?"

Parker gestured around the room, pointing out the altar up front, the candelabras filled with sputtering candles, the large icon of what looked like Rosamund—that saint they all seemed to care so much about. Rows of pews ran the length of the room as the organ music kept playing.

"I know it seems a little weird, but it's tradition." Beth shrugged. "The headmaster gives a daily devotion and then we head off to our first classes. Most of us kind of ignore him, but at least try to look like you're paying attention so you don't get into any trouble."

Parker nodded. She didn't really know what to think about that. Her family had never been the religious type, so she had no clue what to expect. A prayer, maybe? Or some kind of sermon? They wouldn't make her take communion every morning, would they? Or go to confessional?

Glancing around the room, Parker didn't see any goblets filled with wine or grape juice. She didn't see a Bible laid out on the altar or any tapestries hanging from the vaulted ceiling. There was a lectern on a raised platform sitting front and center. And the morning sun streamed in through a big stained-glass window sitting high up on the wall.

A rose window, it looked like, each petal looping around

to form a smooth circle, the panes red and green and glittering gold. The details were too small for Parker to make out from her pew, but if she squinted, she could just see the figures bending and breaking and growing back together, a story told in clockwise scenes.

She leaned forward, but right then the organ music cut out and a door swung open behind her. As if on cue, the students clambered to their feet. Parker, determined not to stick out, followed a couple of seconds behind them.

Turning to the back of the room, she spotted the cause of the fanfare—a tall gray-haired man stood at the entrance, his figure silhouetted in the doorway.

"That's the headmaster," Beth whispered in Parker's right ear, and she nodded with understanding, not taking her eyes off him.

Everyone's eyes followed the man as he made his way down the center aisle. He stood stoically as several students passed, and Parker averted her eyes at the last second, making sure he didn't focus in on her. She didn't want to be singled out on the first day.

Climbing the steps to the dais, the headmaster took his place behind the lectern and paused, his shoulders drawn back, his head held high, his eyes penetrating the crowd of students, checking that all was in place before he opened his mouth to speak in a voice that carried through the chapel.

"For long ago the seed was sown . . ."

"And the good people left to tend the fields and pluck the flowers and reap their hard work's reward."

The students' voices echoed automatically through the room, a patchwork of effort levels as they finished the call-and-response.

"Sit. Sit." The man motioned for them all to relax, and Parker quickly took her spot on the bench, wondering how long she had before they'd expect her to learn and repeat the same verses.

"Good morning," the man greeted them all warmly. "And isn't it a fine morning? A blessed April morning with the harvest nearly upon us."

Parker snuck a peek out of the corner of her eye and saw a few students yawning and fidgeting in their seats, kicking each other's feet as they tried to get one another to break. No one seemed to be hanging on the headmaster's every word. No one except for Brady, who had an oddly enamored look on his face, staring up at the headmaster with an almost unbreakable concentration.

"He's such a suck-up," Beth whispered.

And Parker had to cover her mouth as a snort nearly leapt out of her. She glanced down at her shoes and tried to focus. Tried to keep herself from bursting out in laughter and making a scene as the headmaster kept on with his sermon.

"This time of year always gets me thinking. About

community. About what we can do when we work together. About how we hold each other up and how much stronger we are as one.

"It's no secret that we've had challenges this year. Setbacks and struggles. It has been a long winter. Longer than usual. But do you smell that in the air? Do you sense the warmth creeping in? The days growing longer?

"Spring is upon us. And with spring comes the bloom. Comes the harvest. Comes the fruition of all our hard work."

A couple of over-the-top whoops flew out from the back of the room, and a tremor of laughter followed them. But the headmaster seemed unfazed, raising his voice, speaking with more conviction now as he wound to a close.

"When we work together, nothing can lead us astray. Nothing can uproot our will. We are sowers. We are tenders. We are reapers. And most importantly, we are family.

"Now, let us pray."

He lifted his arms wide and reached out over the room as if to pull them all in under his protection. Then he dipped his head and closed his eyes, everyone around Parker lazily following his lead. She quickly copied the motion, only half listening to the headmaster's words as they filled the room. She was definitely not a pray-er.

"As another spring comes upon us, we give thanks for your blessings. That you've seen us through the cold. That you've kept us fed and in good health. That our brothers and sisters are here by our sides, loving each other and doing your work."

As the headmaster went on, Parker found herself drifting. All this talk about sowing seeds and reaping the harvest went way over her head. At least she wasn't alone in thinking that. But it was too early and too warm in the chapel to have her eyes shut like this.

Her head bobbed forward and then jerked back up as she caught herself at the last second. She could not fall asleep on her first day. She couldn't risk falling out of her pew and causing a commotion, earning herself a new nickname, one even worse than BB.

Carefully, she opened her eyes. She didn't want to seem disrespectful. She didn't want to get on the headmaster's bad side on her very first day. So she kept her head down, staring at the buckles on her shoes. They winked at her, big and shiny and new, reminding her of the pilgrims. But she still couldn't stay awake. And as a yawn stole over her lips, she kept her eyes moving, her gaze wandering farther down the row.

She noticed a few other students who'd grown restless, their feet tap-dancing or playing footsie, their fingers moving to stealthily pinch their neighbors as they kept their heads bowed and their eyes closed.

Parker's attention kept roaming, though, until she hit the end of the row and spotted a boy there sitting by himself, an intentional gap separating him from everyone else. His bleached-blond hair fell in front of his eyes, but he looked to be in deep concentration, his head bowed low over his notebook.

Then his jaw twitched. His bangs fell back as he raised his chin and swiveled around. His eyes locked onto Parker's and he caught her spying.

She flushed, and he grimaced at her. His hand twisted as he capped the bright bottle of nail polish in his lap, his fingers fanned out in front of him as he lazily blew on the fresh coat of paint, a rainbow of colors dotting each of his nails.

"Amen."

Parker blinked and whipped around to face forward, acting like she'd had her head bowed the entire time as she lifted it up with everyone else. She smiled at Beth and snuck a glance back at the nail polish boy, but he'd turned to face the front as well, his mouth puckered as he continued blowing his fingers dry.

"Now," the headmaster said, clapping his hands together and smiling brightly at them all. "I have one last announcement before I dismiss you for your first classes."

The headmaster's eyes began roaming the pews, and Parker's stomach flipped, knowing what he must have in mind. She squirmed lower in her seat, but the chapel was only so big and she couldn't escape his notice for long.

"We have a new student joining us today."

The headmaster found her and lifted his outstretched

hand, encouraging her to stand. It was the last thing Parker wanted to do, but she didn't have a choice. So she got to her feet, slouching, trying to make herself as small as possible. She could feel everyone looking at her, their eyes scurrying across her. Her palms started to sweat. And she worried that she might faint.

But then she felt a hand on her shoulder, pressing down, grounding her. She turned and saw Beth standing there, giving her that perfect smile. And Parker momentarily forgot about what had happened on her first day at her old school. She forgot about feeling like she wouldn't fit in here. She suddenly felt like there was potential in this place. Kindness and warmth. Maybe even a friend.

Her stomach unclenched and she felt her whole body relaxing.

"Everyone," the headmaster said from his lectern, "let's make sure Parker feels welcome here, like a member of our Coronation family."

And as Parker sheepishly raised her hand to wave at them all, she felt a throb of pain. She saw a fresh drop of bright blood bubbling up from the tip of her finger.

She curled her hand into a fist and whipped it back down, smiling through it all, hoping that no one had noticed, that they couldn't see her panic. She looked past everyone and focused on the icon sitting atop the altar, on Rosamund's eyes staring back into hers, boring through her.

And something flashed in them. A flicker of flame. A trick of the light.

Parker blinked and it was gone. But even as everyone started to file out of the chapel, she couldn't shake the strangeness of it. Couldn't forget the fire in her eyes, and the shriek that she now swore she'd heard reverberate against the chapel walls.

CHAPTER
FIVE

"How was your first day?"

Parker lifted her head from her homework and spotted her dad at her bedroom door, his work satchel still slung over his shoulder. It was a sight she'd missed.

"How was *your* first day?" she asked, turning the question right back around on him as she curled her finger into her palm, trying to hide the bandage she'd wrapped around her still-throbbing wound. She didn't want to rehash her day. Didn't want to think about what she'd seen in that painting during chapel.

No. What she'd *imagined*.

Because there hadn't actually been anything there. She'd been tired and overwhelmed by everything new. Her eyes had played a trick on her.

"It was pretty great, actually," Parker's dad said. And she

was relieved to see a real smile lighting up his eyes. He'd been a zombie since losing his last job.

"So what exactly are they making you do?"

Her dad had held a lot of jobs over the years, but none of them ever seemed to make him happy. He'd always said he got bored fast, which wasn't usually a problem since he made sure to have the next job lined up before leaving. However, when he'd been laid off six months ago, he hadn't been able to find anything. And after a month or two of scrambling, he'd kind of given up. That was when the fighting had started, the pressure of unpaid bills piling up, Parker's mom's I-told-you-so hanging in the air between them even though it went unvoiced.

"I'm installing a new security system at the Rosarium," Parker's dad replied. "Wiring their greenhouses and the offices. They've had a few break-ins and some vandalism, and they want to catch whoever's been doing it. I'm kind of surprised they don't already have something set up, but I guess they're just really trusting here. Not like in the city."

No. It wasn't like the city. After only a couple days here, Parker had realized that. But maybe that wasn't a bad thing.

"I'm supposed to tell you that dinner's almost ready," Parker's dad said as he unshouldered his bag. "Meet you down there."

Parker got up from her desk and padded out of the room and down the stairs—the two-floor thing was going to take some getting used to. As she made her way into the kitchen, the scent of rosemary and garlic hung in the air. She eyed the potatoes spitting and sizzling on the stove top. She wanted to reach out and fork one, but her mom shot her a look and she backed away.

"Can you get the table set?" she asked, turning back to the stove.

"On it," Parker said automatically, happy to fall back into her usual role. Relieved that it felt like old times again.

It took her a couple of tries to find the right cabinets, but eventually she had enough plates, forks, knives, and glasses for them all. They had a separate dining room in this house, but it felt weird to eat in something like that, so Parker set everything out in the breakfast nook, lining it all up until it looked perfect.

Tonight was special. It was their first home-cooked meal.

"Did you make my favorite?" her dad said, strolling into the kitchen. He'd thrown on a T-shirt to replace his work button-down. He smiled big at Parker's mom, moving behind the counter to wrap his arms around her waist. He hugged her close and then kissed her on the cheek.

"Steak and potatoes," Parker's mom replied, a trill in her voice. "Just the way you like it."

Parker's dad inhaled deeply and then let her mom go slowly.

"With lots of garlic. Here, let me help you with those." He scooped up two of the serving dishes and made his way to the table. Parker's mom undid her apron and followed with the salad, a skip in her step, like she was a teenager again. Usually, it would have grossed Parker out to catch her parents acting all lovey-dovey, but this moment in the kitchen made her heart soar. Told her that they'd made the right decision in coming here.

"So you never told me how *your* first day went," Parker's dad said as they all sat down at the kitchen table.

"Did Mrs. York's son end up giving you the tour?" Parker's mom asked.

"He was supposed to," Parker replied as she spooned a few potatoes onto her plate. "But he never showed up."

"That doesn't sound right." Parker's mom frowned. "I should talk to his mom. See if—"

"It's fine." Parker cut her off. She probably shouldn't have brought up Brady's no-show in the first place. She didn't want to get him in trouble. He was a jerk. Ratting him out to Mrs. York would only make him mad. She didn't need that kind of target on her back.

"Actually, his sister took me around instead."

"And was everyone nice?" Parker's mom asked without skipping a beat.

"They were," Parker said. But then she really thought about it.

Apart from Brady standing her up and that kid grimacing at her during chapel, everyone had been nice to her. Beth in particular. But she didn't know if that was genuine or not. She knew better than to trust someone like Beth. Brady had already shown his true colors. It wouldn't surprise Parker if his sister ended up turning out the same way. If the girl was just like Callie underneath all that smile.

"There was a weird prayer thing to start the day," Parker remembered, shifting the conversation. "But I guess it goes with the school."

"The Sowers," Parker's mom nodded, as if it were obvious.

"The what?" her dad asked, pausing between bites. And Parker was glad that she wasn't the only one in the dark.

"Didn't you all read the information packet?"

Parker's mom glanced between them both before rolling her eyes playfully.

"Please, enlighten us," Parker's dad joked.

"The Sowers. It's like their—" And Parker's mom paused for a moment, trying to find the right word. "It's not a cult. But not a full religion either. It's kind of like their way of life. Their philosophy."

Parker raised her eyebrows, not understanding any of it.

"It's like the Quakers. Or the Shakers. Or something."

Parker's mom gave up when neither Parker nor her dad seemed to pick up on what she was saying.

"They believe in brotherly love and family and hard work and respect." Parker's mom waved their doubtful stares away. "You get the gist. It's harmless. And probably some values that we could all use a refresher course on."

47

"As long as they're not trying to brainwash anyone," Parker's dad chuckled.

And then the kitchen grew quiet as they focused on their meal, ice tinkling in their glasses, knives and forks clinking against their plates. Parker didn't know how her mom had pulled it all together. She'd probably put in a full day of work at her data entry job, one they were lucky she'd been able to move remote. And with all the unpacking and organizing she'd been doing, Parker didn't know how she wasn't ready to drop.

"Speaking of school." Parker's mom brightened. "I got the newsletter this morning and it looks like tennis tryouts are at the end of the week. Isn't that perfect timing?"

Parker froze, her fork suspended in midair.

"I'm sure you're dying to break out your racket and get back on the court."

Parker hadn't thought about tennis for the last two days. And she didn't want to. Not when it made her think of Dani. Something lurched in her gut, and she wondered if she'd ever want to pick up a racket again.

"Sounds great."

Parker un-paused, lifting her fork the rest of the way to her mouth. She took her time chewing and then swallowed, forcing a smile that she hoped would fool her parents.

"Okay if I head up to my room?" she asked. "I've got some homework to finish up."

"You can go," Parker's dad dismissed her, and she got up from the table, dropping her plate in the sink on her way out.

As she climbed the stairs, her parents' voices bubbled up beneath her, laughing and happy and in love. And Parker was glad to give them this moment alone.

Slipping into her bedroom, Parker closed the door. She leaned against it, her gaze sweeping the floor, landing on the box that she knew would still be there. She'd unpacked almost everything, but she'd purposely left this alone, all her tennis gear sealed away inside. Her racket and bag. The tubes of unopened balls. Her lucky visor and bright-pink tennis shoes. The ones she'd gotten to match Dani's. It felt like too much to play without her now.

Turning her back on the box, Parker plopped down in her desk chair. She took her phone out and flipped through her apps, but Dani hadn't posted anything since the night they'd gotten caught. Had her parents taken her phone? After she'd sent Parker all those messages? Was that a part of her grounding? The longer she'd gone without talking to Dani, the more real it felt. She'd lost her best friend.

Parker clicked through to her texts and pulled up her last conversation with Dani. Her eyes slid over the words, not wanting to relive them. But she couldn't delete them either. She couldn't let herself off the hook that easily. Her fingers hovered over the keyboard, trying to figure out what to say. What she *could* say.

But there was nothing. No magic words for saving a friendship. And no point in even trying now that she was in Coronation.

She clicked out of her messages and dropped her phone on her books. Homework was at least one productive thing she could do right now. Picking up a pencil, she moved to get back to her assignment. But as she went to turn the page, she stopped, not understanding what she was looking at. There was a card sitting there on top of her open textbook. She hadn't noticed it when she'd walked in, but it definitely hadn't been there before.

Slowly, Parker picked it up, massaging the thick stock between her fingertips. She examined the illustration on the front. Someone had obviously spent a lot of time on it. It was a drawing of a rose, its petals unfurling in crimson waves, the thorns sticking out of its long stem at deadly angles.

But the flower wasn't the star of the picture. That belonged to the bright emerald insect perched on the lip of the rose's blossom. It pulsed with life, as if it were hovering like a hummingbird there in the drawing. Its outer shell glimmered like a precious stone, and Parker had to stop herself from touching it, afraid that she might smear the ink of the anonymous artist.

Carefully, she opened the card, looking for the message inside. But as she read the words written there, she dropped it, her fingers stinging as if she'd just grabbed a whole bunch of roses by the thorns. She jumped to her feet and whirled around. Her gaze fell on the window. Had someone climbed through it while they'd been eating dinner?

It was the only explanation. The only way that note could have gotten up here.

Parker crossed the room, but the window was still locked. She peered into the backyard anyway and saw movement. Someone crouching in the bushes. She gasped.

But then just as quickly, she realized it was only one of Mrs. York's men. A gardener tending to the flowers, the Rosarium's logo emblazoned there across his chest.

He wouldn't have left her something like this.

But then who would have?

Parker pulled her curtains shut, but that didn't help. She couldn't stop her trembling as she moved back to her desk and picked up the card. A new set of chills ran through her as she reread the words.

You don't belong here.

And then in even bigger letters underneath that:

LEAVE.

51

CHAPTER
SIX

What was she doing here? Why had she agreed to come along?

Parker's head pinged back and forth, tracking the movement of the ball, following every shot. Her fingers tightened around her own racket and her stomach lurched as the point ended.

"It's almost our turn," Beth said, out of breath with excitement before they'd even started playing.

Parker turned and gave the girl a weak smile. She hadn't planned on trying out, but when she'd come home from school the day before, she'd found her tennis equipment sitting out on her bed, waiting for her. Her mom had unearthed it from its sealed moving box, which meant that Parker'd had to bring it to school with her today. If she hadn't, it would have raised too many questions. And Parker did not need her mom poking around about why she didn't want to play tennis anymore.

Her plan had been to leave her stuff in her locker and hide out after school until her mom came to pick her up. Then she would just have to pretend that she hadn't made the team. That the other girls were too good and that she'd been rusty during tryouts. Everyone had bad days.

But Beth had spotted her that morning and leapt and squealed in the hallway because she was trying out for the team, too. And wouldn't it be the best if they both made it and got to play together?

Parker hadn't had the heart to let Beth down. While something about the girl still seemed a little too good to be true, Parker couldn't deny the fact that Beth had stuck by her side for the past week. She hadn't abandoned Parker after that first tour. She hadn't played any tricks on her or made fun of her clothes. She'd sat next to her at lunch. They'd worked on their homework together in the library. Beth had even introduced Parker to just about everyone she knew, always enthusiastic about it. Always bright and bubbly. Always flashing that perfect smile.

So here Parker was, racket in hand, satisfying one guilty conscience, but at the same time, trying to ignore another. She wiped her palms on her tennis skirt, feeling the nerves already. She couldn't remember the last time she'd played without Dani.

"Which side do you want to take?"

Beth's question caught Parker off guard. She had to think about it. She'd always played the deuce side. Dani had the power. Her forehand streaked through the court. Parker was a backhander, solid with her strokes. Consistent. She didn't overpower her opponents. She wore them down over time. That combination had always been one of their strengths.

"I can play the ad side," Parker said, surprising herself with the decision. "Let's do this."

Beth gave her a high five before skipping across the court. Parker followed, swinging her racket, trying to loosen her arms and get all her muscles warmed up. This was just a hitting drill to see their mechanics, but Parker worried that she might not remember what to do. At least Beth hadn't seen her play before. She wouldn't have any expectations.

"Ready?" the coach called from across the court. And then, without waiting for an answer, she started feeding them balls.

The first went to Beth, a soft floater that sat up right in her strike zone. Parker watched, impressed as Beth shuffled her feet easily and hit the ball right back with a smooth, practiced swing.

"Now you."

Parker froze as the coach hit the next ball to her. Her elbows wouldn't move. They were pinned to her sides, handcuffing her swing. And the ball was getting closer. It was right on her. If she didn't do something, she was going to miss it. She was going to choke.

But then, as the ball bounced, something in Parker unlocked. Her legs moved into position and her arm swung back. She concentrated on the ball, watching it the whole way in. She stayed low and steady, muscle memory taking over. And she snapped a clean forehand down the line.

The shot sounded good coming off her racket. That perfect strum of string meeting ball. The swing rolled through her arm, her follow-through finishing up as her shoulder turned. It felt so easy. So right. It felt like home.

The coach began feeding the balls faster then, challenging Beth and Parker more with each hit. But they could handle it. They both could play. They got into a rally, Parker's experience coming out. She started calling for the ball, telling Beth what to do and where to stand. Urging her to rush the net whenever they hit the ball deep and had the advantage.

After a particularly deft volley, Parker watched as the coach scrambled to get the ball back, barely getting her racket on it. The ball soared up in the air, a lob that didn't have enough on it to get over Parker's head at the net. She pulled her racket back, ready to let loose a crushing, swinging volley to finish the point. But as the ball floated down toward her, a memory flashed in front of her eyes. She saw Dani taking the same shot, rocketing the ball past their opponents, clinching last summer's city championship with the winner.

How was she able to let someone else take her place so quickly?

Parker blinked, coming back to the present too late. The ball was already on her. She didn't have time to adjust. Unbalanced, she swung and launched the ball high into the air, sending it sailing over the back fence, miles long.

"I'll get it," Parker exclaimed, her cheeks burning. She dropped her racket and took off, running away from both the missed shot and the memory.

She sprinted off the courts and turned to follow the fence. She wasn't sure where exactly she had hit the ball, and part of her didn't care. Part of her just wanted to run, to be away from the court. Just to have a few minutes to collect herself. The school campus was huge, and the tennis facility was situated in a clearing that she hadn't explored yet. Trees towered around it and blocked the view. But it wasn't so dense that she couldn't see through it. Arriving at the spot where she thought she'd hit the ball out, Parker waded in.

The long grass parted as she picked her way through the undergrowth, her eyes peeled for any sign of bright-yellow fuzz. She'd rocketed that thing, an easy put away that she'd mis-hit terribly. It could be anywhere back here.

She hadn't wanted to try out, she reminded herself. She'd known it would be hard. And now here was the proof. Evidence that she couldn't do it without Dani. She could focus for a few points. Could get into a groove. But the memories were there, ready to come out at any second. The guilt. The betrayal.

Parker tried to push the thoughts out of her head, but she could feel the echo of that swing in her arm. How the shot had jolted through her bones, an uncomfortable reminder of her failures. Of her limitations.

Shaking her head, she kept moving and was surprised when she broke through the tree line, coming out into what she quickly realized was a huge garden. She could smell it even before she saw it.

All around her, bushes and shrubs and topiaries spread their green leaves in every direction. But there was an order to it all. Plants grouped together in bunches. Neat paths laid out between rows of flower beds. Small signs stuck in the ground that called out what specifically was planted where.

Parker's hand rose to cover her mouth as she took it all in. How had no one told her about this place? It was straight out of a fairy tale.

Instantly, Parker forgot why she'd come back here in the first place. She wandered along one of the paths. There didn't seem to be anyone around. All she could hear was the chirping of birds and the gurgle of a nearby fountain. It was still too early for the flowers to have bloomed, but she could see the signs of spring to come. She squinted to read some of the signs, but she didn't recognize any of the names.

Chinensis. Grandiflora. Floribunda. Damascena.

She got to the end of the path and started down a new one, completely mesmerized.

The bushes were arranged in a circle, the unopened blossoms fat polka dots of purest white peeking out through the green, waiting to bloom. If that hadn't given it away, then the thorns would have.

Roses.

Parker bent over, awestruck by the flowers. This close, she could pick up their sweet scent, delicate and bright and subtle. She wondered how they'd look once they unfurled their petals. How their smell might intensify.

"They'll be blooming in no time," a voice said, startling Parker. She popped up straight and almost fell over as an old woman materialized right behind her, walking out of a shrub as if she'd just come to life.

"You're allowed to look," the woman said, a disarming smile curving her lips upward. She had a round face, wrinkled but still soft. The hem of her long navy robe nipped at the blades of grass, and she'd tucked her short hair behind her ears.

With a soft thud, she set a bucket down on the ground and rummaged through it, pulling out a small pair of shears.

"I'm Sister Florence," the woman said. "I see that the *Rosa alba* have caught your eye."

The sharp pincers clicked open and closed in her hands as she turned and eyed the bush Parker had been examining.

"The what?" Parker stuttered. And only when the woman

58

gestured toward the ground did Parker see the sign there with the Latin name scrawled out in neat letters.

"The White Rose of York," the woman explained as she leaned in, pulling a few stems forward to get a closer look. "It's one of our finest specimens."

She took her time pulling stalk after stalk to her. And then, with a deft chop, she sheared one off at its base.

"What are you doing?" Parker cried out, her cheeks reddening as she realized how silly she must sound. They were only flowers. Why should she care so much?

"Pruning," the woman said without taking her eyes off the roses. "You have to take out the weak and broken stalks so the rest of them can grow strong."

The woman clipped three more stalks and then spun back around to her bucket. She tossed the flower remains inside and set her shears down as well. Then she knelt and her whole hand disappeared, coming out a moment later with a pile of fine, soot-colored dirt. She returned to the rosebush and carefully sprinkled the dirt over the ground.

"And that's fertilizer?" Parker asked, her uncertainty disappearing as the woman nodded and continued her work, patting the mixture down, gently massaging it into the earth.

"Do you know the history of the Wars of the Roses?" Sister Florence asked, and Parker mumbled out a quick no.

"It was a series of civil wars that took place in England in the fifteenth century," the woman explained. "A fight for the crown. The red rose of Lancaster versus the white rose of York."

The woman looked up at Parker, holding her gaze for a few moments before turning back to the bushes, inspecting them closely.

"The Yorks ended up losing that fight, but we still have their rose to remember them by."

Sister Florence's smile faltered for a second, but then came back as she got to her feet, clapping her hands together to shake off the loose dirt. She grabbed her bucket and prepared to move along to the next row of plants.

Parker wanted to stop her. She wanted to follow the woman. Wanted to learn more about all of this. But she knew that she couldn't hang out here all day. She knew that Beth was probably wondering where she'd gone. And as much as she didn't want to play tennis, she also didn't want to abandon her newest—and maybe only—friend.

"Can I come back?" The question popped out of Parker's mouth before she realized it. "And you can show me more?" She bit her bottom lip and waited. She didn't know why this suddenly interested her so much. Horticulture, or whatever it was called. But it did.

"You can find me here every afternoon."

With that, Sister Florence lifted her bucket off the ground and hobbled down the row, leaving Parker to find her own way back to the tennis courts.

CHAPTER
SEVEN

A bee hummed nearby, catching Parker's attention as she stood on the sidewalk waiting for her mother. Her gaze drifted, searching until she spotted the insect's furry yellow body zipping through the air. It dipped and rose as it followed a curlicue path. And then, eventually, it found its target and landed on a window box, disappearing into the flower buds sprouting there. The petals shook, and the bee crawled out a few seconds later, taking off again, its legs and wings coated in a fine dust, ready for pollination.

It reminded Parker of the school garden. Of the life that seemed ready to burst all around Coronation, from the rosebushes surrounding her house to every single shop here on Main Street that had flowerpots sitting out front. The light felt brighter here. The air, if it was possible, seemed to be getting sweeter. It felt right.

But at the same time, it felt off. Too neat. Too easy. And Parker couldn't help wondering if there was an ugliness hidden beneath Coronation's polish.

Perhaps the thought would never have even occurred to her if not for the drawing. The metallic-green insect that someone had left on her desk. The threat that had come with it.

Her stomach lurched. She still had no idea who had left it for her. Who would want to scare her like that? Why had they come after her in the first place? Because she was the new girl? Because they didn't think she belonged in their fancy town?

She'd dealt with bullies at her old school. But this was different. She didn't know who was coming after her. Which meant that she didn't know who she could trust. It could have been Brady or Beth or someone she hadn't even met yet.

"So what's next?" Parker's mom asked, appearing right next to Parker on the sidewalk, startling her out of her daze.

"I think we're done," Parker replied as she took out the wrinkled shopping list that her mom had handed her that morning. "We've got extras of my uniform. And school supplies. And new shoes."

Parker ticked it all off. She felt guilty that they were spending so much on her all at once, but her mom had insisted on getting her set up. They couldn't live on Mrs. York's kindness for too long. And her father had gotten a decent stipend from his new job for moving expenses.

"Now all we need is your dad," Parker's mom said, glancing

up and down the street. "Can you run this to the car while I find him? He gets distracted easily."

Parker nodded as she took the bags from her mom and grabbed the keys. She was happy for the distraction, for a way to get out of her head before she spiraled too badly.

Walking down the sidewalk, the keys jingling in her hand, Parker passed a pharmacy and two cafés, all local. She was kind of surprised that there weren't any chains. They existed when you got outside of town, but here in the center of it, everything wore the same rustic charm of clapboard shutters, artfully climbing ivy, stone walls, and flagstone sidewalks.

But even though it looked old, nothing had faded. Every store had a fresh coat of paint. Every front window had been wiped clean and crystal clear. Strings of fairy lights crisscrossed overhead, and Parker could imagine how it would all look at night. The soft glow and hum. People spilling out into the street, passing from shop to shop, their chatter light and happy and warm. It felt like walking onto a movie set. The perfect little town.

Getting to the car, Parker unlocked it with the key fob and set everything in the back. She figured she should probably wait there for her parents, but as she leaned against the trunk, a tingle pricked at the back of her neck.

She stood up and looked around, searching for that something that had her on edge. And then she spotted him. A boy staring at her from across the street, his gaze steady and unmistakable. He had a black beanie pulled over his head, but she recognized the tips of his bleached-blond hair that stuck out from beneath. The glint of his now bright-blue nails. He had that same grimace on his face as he lifted a hand in her direction. But instead of waving at her, he threw something down on the ground.

A crack split through the quiet Main Street air, and Parker jumped, her heart suddenly racing in her chest. She watched as the boy lifted his hand again and launched what she realized must be a firecracker in her direction. It landed in the middle of the road and went off, as loud as a gunshot.

Parker flinched once more, but she managed to stand her ground. She leveled her gaze at the boy, wondering what he could possibly want with her.

He raised his hand again, but this time it was empty. Instead of tossing another firework at her, he simply waved, the light twinkling off his bright-blue nails as he fanned them in her direction. He gave her one last grimace, and then he turned, taking off down the street.

But Parker wasn't going to let him go that easily. She didn't waste a second as she stepped down from the curb and took off running after him. She'd seen the boy a couple of times since that first day at chapel. But only in passing. He hadn't appeared in any of her classes, and she still didn't know his name or what his deal was. She didn't know anything about him or why he'd been staring at her. But she was going to find out.

Picking up her pace, Parker tried to catch up. It was hard, though. The boy kept his distance, weaving around street signs and fire hydrants, ducking behind large vases of flowers so that Parker lost sight of him.

But as evasive as he was, it also seemed like he wanted her to follow him. Every block or two he'd sneak a quick look over his shoulder before pressing on.

Parker tailed him like this for a few minutes, worrying that she'd run out of Main Street real estate. But then, suddenly, the boy darted down an alleyway. Parker charged forward, sure she'd caught up to him finally. But when she turned the corner, he was nowhere in sight.

No one was there at all. Just a wall staring back at her, an advertisement covering every inch of it.

But there was more to it, Parker realized quickly. Someone had painted over the original billboard and created their own mural.

Hundreds of brilliant green shapes swarmed in front of Parker, so thick they could block out the sun. And in the center of the storm, a woman floated in midair, her silhouette inky black.

Parker took a step forward and homed in on one of the green things. It looked familiar, but she couldn't figure out exactly what it was until—

She saw the two little antennae. And the delicate, translucent wings.

She took a quick step back and looked at the mural again, the splashes of spray paint glinting in the light. It was just like the card someone had left on her desk. The illustration was almost identical, the insects swirling in a tornado, protecting their queen.

Or were they attacking her?

"What are you doing here?" Parker's dad's voice came up from behind her, startling her.

"I—" Parker stuttered, not knowing what to say. "Mom was looking for you."

"Sorry about that," Parker's dad apologized sheepishly. "I know I disappeared on you all. I wanted to check this out, though. See what the Yorks are up against?"

Parker's brow furrowed as she looked at her dad.

"See," her dad went on, pointing up at the mural as if it was evidence. "This is why the Yorks hired me. To find out who's been vandalizing them. You can't go around damaging private property and expect to get away with it."

Except, Parker suddenly realized, that was exactly what she had done. Or, at least, that had been the plan. With Dani and those tennis rackets. What would her dad say if he knew?

"It's not that big a deal, is it?" Parker asked, more coming to her own defense than the mural artist's. "I think it looks pretty cool actually. And it's not hurting anyone."

"Mrs. York paid money to put up that ad," Parker's dad explained patiently. "And now it's ruined."

Parker turned back to the mural and squinted. Then she saw it. The faint image underneath all the swirling insects. Her new neighbor's smiling face, a bunch of roses clutched in one hand.

"Come on," Parker's dad said, his hand finding his daughter's shoulder. "Your mom's probably waiting for us at the car."

Parker's dad turned to head back, but Parker lingered for a couple more seconds, examining the graffiti. She had a pretty good idea of who was behind it. Why else would he have wanted her to see it? But did that also mean he was the one who'd left her that card? Had that threat been his? And had he done it again that afternoon?

You don't belong here.

LEAVE.

The words came back to Parker. But this time they didn't scare her. They made her angry. Parker didn't know what to think about the boy. She didn't even know his name. But now that she had a lead, she was going to find out. And she was going to make sure he knew not to mess with her.

Sliding her phone out, Parker took a quick photo of the wall.

She was tired of being the new girl. Tired of people picking on her just because they could. Callie and everyone else had walked all over her at her old school, and she wasn't going to let that happen to her here.

CHAPTER
EIGHT

Walking to school on Monday morning, Parker could sense something different in the air, a subtle shift that she couldn't quite put her finger on. But it was there all the same, noticeable as a grain of sand in her shoe, rubbing with every step that she took.

It might have been that she had plans today. A mission. She was going to find the bleached-blond boy and figure out what he wanted with her. Why he'd left her that note. Why he'd led her to that mural. What the green insects meant. She'd corner him after chapel and make him talk to her. She didn't care if she was late to class. She needed to know. And she needed to put an end to it.

Looking up, Parker was surprised to see that she'd already made it to school. The mile walk had flown by. She was earlier than usual, which was part of her plan. She'd stow her books in her locker and head to the chapel so that she could pick out a seat in the back. That way the boy couldn't sneak out without her noticing.

She'd catch him for sure.

Except, as Parker made her way down the empty school hallway, she felt her confidence waning. She felt alone. Dani had always been the strong one. The one who never backed down from a confrontation.

Parker wished she had her best friend there with her. She wished she could lean on her for support. She could use a pep talk. And the backup in case things went badly. She could use . . .

Suddenly, a door crashed open behind Parker. She didn't have a second to react. To run or shout or throw a punch. Before she knew it, a pair of hands had reached out and grabbed her, dragging her through the doorway of an empty classroom.

"What the—" Parker managed to shout, the shock wearing off as her reflex to fight kicked in. To bite and scream and claw her way to freedom. But a hand quickly clamped over her mouth, shutting her up and causing her panic to rise.

It felt like she was suffocating, her brain getting fuzzier every second. She could hear the blood pumping into her head, filling her ears. Was it about to start dribbling out of her nose? Was she about to die?

"I'm not going to hurt you," a voice whispered into her ear.

But she didn't believe it. She kept struggling, stamping her feet, trying to land a blow so that her attacker would be forced to let her go.

"I just need to talk to you. Before it's too late."

Parker kept wriggling, kept trying to scream. Her eyes strayed down to that hand clamped over her mouth, those fingers pressed over her lips, the bright-blue nail polish winking at her—and she stopped. She forced herself to swallow her protest. And as she calmed down, the boy's grip slowly loosened.

"It's you," Parker seethed as she turned to face the bleached-blond boy.

She knew that she should have run out of there right then. She should have made a break for safety. But she'd been looking for him. And she didn't want to miss her chance to finally get some answers.

"Why have you been threatening me?" Parker demanded. "What did I ever do to you?"

"It's happening," the boy mumbled, completely ignoring her question. And Parker saw how lost he was in his own frenzy.

"It's happening today," he repeated himself. "I thought I had more time."

"Had more time for what?" Parker asked.

He looked at her then, eyeballing her as if she'd dragged him in here and not the other way around.

"What's happening?" Parker tried again.

"The Bloom," he whispered, as if that made things any clearer. "Can't you smell it?"

70

Parker paused then, remembering how something had felt different that morning.

Now that she thought about it, she had noticed that the rosebushes in front of her house had opened up overnight, the blossoms big and lovely. And if those had bloomed, then they must have done the same across town. The flowers at the Rosarium. The ones in the window boxes lining Main Street. The bushes and trees and shrubs in the school garden. They must have all come to life. Parker knew because she could smell it in the air. The aroma was everywhere.

But why did that matter? Flowers bloomed in spring. It certainly didn't warrant a kidnapping.

"You have to get out of here," the boy begged her, his voice trembling, his gaze unfocused, as if he were reliving some nightmare. "You have to go. Now. Leave."

The last word sent shivers down Parker's back. Made it clear that her suspicions were right.

He was the one who had left her that note. Who had threatened her. But before she could call him on it, his hands shot out and grabbed both of her wrists, shaking her to the bone.

"It's not safe for you here."

"Let go of me!" Parker shouted, and she pulled herself free, backing away toward the door.

The boy opened his mouth again, but right then, Parker heard someone calling her name.

"Parker? Are you there?"

Beth.

Parker turned toward the door, so ready to get out of there and away from this boy who seemed unhinged.

"Hold on tight."

His words cut through her. The intensity behind them was scary. Where he'd been frightened before, his message resounded with a seriousness now. A finality. A warning.

"Whatever you do, don't let go. Don't fall down."

"What?"

Parker was so confused.

"Don't let Rosie win."

His hands shook with every single word. And then, just as suddenly as he'd pulled her into that room, he disappeared, slipping out a back door that Parker hadn't even realized was there, leaving her to wonder what he'd been talking about.

"Parker? Are you in there?" Beth's voice carried through the door as she knocked on the other side. "Is everything okay?"

Trying to compose herself as best she could, Parker ran her fingers through her hair and then opened the door.

"I'm fine. I just got a little lost." Parker shrugged and tried to look embarrassed. For some reason, she didn't want to tell Beth about the boy. About his cryptic warning. His threats. It was weird any way she looked at it, and she didn't want Beth to think that she couldn't handle things herself.

72

"You sure?" Beth didn't seem to be buying it, but Parker knew how to breeze past it.

"Were you looking for me? Did you need something?"

Beth brightened at the request, her hands fidgeting behind her back like she could barely contain herself. Then she leapt forward, a ring of flowers appearing in her grip. A crown, Parker realized, as the girl looped it over her head.

"Happy Bloom," Beth cheered. And then the girl took Parker's arm and dragged her down the hall.

CHAPTER
NINE

"What are you doing?" Parker squealed, trying her best to keep up as Beth pulled her along down the hallway.

"You'll see," Beth giggled, shooting a look over her shoulder before speeding up, causing Parker to stumble.

But she knew how to shuffle and adjust her feet. Tennis had taught her how to keep her balance. And with only a few steps, she was back up and running, her attention driven forward, trying to work out where Beth was leading her.

The mystery only intensified as they flew past the chapel and the cafeteria and the main offices. Then they broke out of the building altogether, their feet hitting the back lawn, slipping through the green grass, which was still damp with dew. They weaved through the stream of students making their way down the slope, and Parker noticed that all the girls had flowers arranged in their braids, too. Roses and lilacs and irises, brilliant in the morning light. And the boys wore the same, only theirs were tucked into buttonholes or pinned onto their lapels. Everyone seemed cheerful. Some girls were even dancing.

"Come on," Beth said. "We don't want to miss it."

She tugged Parker's arm again, pulling her faster through the crowd. That was when Parker finally realized where they were headed.

The aroma hit her as soon as she passed underneath the entrance archway. The perfume filled the air, making Parker a little woozy with its sweetness. If possible, the gardens were even more beautiful than before. Every bush and tree and stem seemed to have blossomed all at once, their vibrant flowers offered up like shining jewels, precious and rare. Parker couldn't stop marveling at it. Had Sister Florence really done all of this?

"Welcome to the Bloom Festival." Beth's voice trilled with excitement as she threw her arms wide and spun around in a circle. "Isn't it amazing?"

"It's incredible," Parker gaped, doing a twirl, too, just because she wanted to take it all in.

She'd only seen a portion of the gardens her first time through. Just a few rows, really. This was so much more. This felt like she was on the grounds of some European palace, like the queen would walk by at any moment and expect her to curtsy.

Five paths shot out under her like sunbeams, blazing trails through the flower beds and bushes and hedges and trees. She wanted to explore them all.

"This way."

Beth's fingers wound their way around Parker's wrist again, but this time it was an invitation. She waited for Parker to join her, and then led her down the middle path.

"Every spring we celebrate the first bloom," Beth explained. "I told you about it. Remember? When I showed you around that first day?"

Parker did remember. Vaguely.

"But didn't that have to do with that saint? Rose-or-something?"

"Rosamund," Beth corrected her. "That's who we're celebrating. She helped the original settlers plant their first fields. She's the reason they had food to eat. The reason they survived after that first winter."

"But where did she come from?" Parker had been wondering this. She couldn't have appeared out of thin air, could she?

"It's just a story," Beth laughed.

"But stories are usually based on something true."

"Well, I guess if you asked the historians, they'd tell you that she wandered over from another colony. She got lost or was kicked out or something. But she'd lived here long enough to know how to survive off the land."

That all made sense to Parker, even if it wasn't the most fantastic of origin stories.

"But the legends are different," Beth went on. "They say that she sprang from the single rose the settlers had managed to bring over from England. The rose that they'd kept alive over the long voyage and planted right here in the middle of the gardens."

The girls spilled out into a small clearing then, and Parker glanced around, hoping that she might catch sight of the fabled flower.

"Oh, it's not here," Beth said, as if reading her thoughts.

Of course it wouldn't be. What kind of flower could have survived for hundreds of years?

"It's in there," Beth said, pointing to a wall of impenetrable leaves and flowers, the tall hedges looking like something straight out of Wonderland. "At the very center of the maze."

There was a full-on hedge maze in here? In addition to the acres of flowers and shrubs and trees and fountains and ponds?

Now Parker knew that Sister Florence couldn't possibly have tended to all of this by herself. They must have an entire staff of gardeners working full-time. Or maybe there was an elective that Parker had missed in the school's course catalog?

"Come on, let's get some food," Beth said.

Again, Parker felt a tug at her arm and Beth pulled her

toward the middle of the clearing, where someone had set up tables holding snacks and a large punch bowl. Teachers were handing out plates and cups to all the students who were streaming in through the different paths.

As Parker waited in line, the scent from the flowers tickled her nose again. She inhaled deeply, letting it fill her up and overpower her. With the sun shining down, she felt warm and happy and woozy. The worries that had been playing on her mind that morning suddenly seemed trivial. Even the boy with the nail polish. His threats or warnings or whatever. It all felt like it didn't matter anymore. She was ready to celebrate. Because it wasn't just the flowers blooming. Her life was starting over. And as scared as she'd been to leave everything she'd known behind, it had all worked out. She hadn't embarrassed herself beyond repair on her first day of school. Her parents were talking. They hadn't even fought once since the move. They had a big house to live in. And a close-knit community that had welcomed them in—a picturesque town where nothing ever seemed to go wrong. She kind of fit in here. And she'd actually made a new friend.

Parker peeked over at Beth, and it shocked her to think that she could get along with someone like her. Someone popular and pretty and poised. Someone way out of her league in terms of social status. She realized, suddenly, that she trusted the girl. That maybe they'd even be best friends one day.

Hold on tight. Don't fall down.

The boy's warning flitted into Parker's head, but she pushed it down. She took a deep breath and then another. She relaxed into the breaths.

This time she could pick out the scent of the roses from the rest of the bouquet, their sweetness traveling down into her lungs and then spreading out through her entire body. She could feel every one of her muscles relaxing, her doubts slipping away. Life was perfect now. She had absolutely nothing to worry about.

"Welcome, everyone."

The familiar voice of the headmaster resounded through the clearing, and Parker turned to see him standing in the middle of it all.

"Gather around."

He raised his arms and beckoned them all to join him. The students moved automatically to form a circle that encompassed him as if they'd done this hundreds of times before.

"It's so good to see all of you this morning. My wife and I . . ." The crowd parted then, and someone moved to join the headmaster in the middle—a woman Parker quickly recognized as Mrs. York, her straight blond hair paired with an effortlessly exquisite sundress.

". . . We look forward to this celebration every year," Mrs. York said, placing her hand lightly on the headmaster's shoulder. "It means so much to us and the entire community."

Parker looked around the circle and realized that it wasn't

made up of just Coronation Country Day students and staff. There were faces from all over town. Younger brothers and sisters. Adults she knew must have been parents and former students. People she didn't recognize at all.

"Now, shall we kick things off and crown this year's Rose Duchess?"

A cheer went up around the crowd, so loud it almost drowned out the headmaster's words. Turning, Parker looked for Beth, hoping for an explanation, but the girl was already moving forward, leaving her behind for the first time that day.

Then, just when Parker thought Beth had forgotten about her altogether, the girl turned and smiled.

"Come on. You don't want to miss your chance at being named Rose Duchess."

CHAPTER
TEN

As they pushed their way through the crowd, Parker kept her eyes on Beth's back. She'd never been the girly type, never interested in pageants or tiaras or playing princess as a kid. But something about this tugged at her.

The Rose Duchess.

How did they go about choosing who'd get the title? Would it go to the prettiest girl? Would they have to perform a talent and then be judged by the audience? Would it be a quiz on the town's history?

In any case, Parker didn't stand much of a chance. She'd just moved to Coronation, and she definitely wasn't the best-looking girl. She only had the one thing that she was really good at—tennis. But she couldn't show off her skills without her racket. She didn't stand a chance.

It could be fun to compete, though. And she'd be able to

cheer on Beth, who probably had a good chance at winning. Parker could picture a crown on the girl's head, nestled in her long blond hair.

As they came out of the crowd, Parker and Beth joined the rest of the hopeful girls in a clump off to the side from where the headmaster and Mrs. York stood. There were about fifty of them from all four grades at the high school. They jostled each other in their excitement, doing last-minute fixes on each other's hair, repositioning flower crowns and retying the ribbons some of them wore around their wrists. Beth turned to Parker and mimicked the preening, combing her fingers through the ends of Parker's locks, loosening any tangles that might have formed since that morning.

"You don't have to worry about me," Parker said, blushing as she pushed Beth's hands away.

"It's anyone's game to win," Beth assured her, though Parker doubted that. "You never know who Rosamund will choose."

Rosamund?

Before Parker could say anything back, the headmaster's voice filled the air again.

"To celebrate each year's Bloom, we call upon Rosamund to choose a worthy representative from among our girls. Someone who exudes light and determination. Someone who understands charity and what it means to give. Someone who will be a beacon of hope for our community throughout the new year."

The headmaster paused as everyone clapped.

"We've had some surprise winners in the past," he continued once the crowd had quieted back down. "But they've never failed us. Rosamund always chooses wisely. For long ago the seed was sown . . ."

As the now-familiar call-and-response came out of the headmaster's mouth, Parker found herself joining in for the first time

"And the good people left to tend the fields and pluck the flowers and reap their hard work's reward."

The headmaster clapped his hands together once and grinned out at everyone assembled, a proud father. He motioned to the side and two men came forward, carrying what looked like a human-sized Chia Pet. They set it right next to the headmaster and moved away.

That was when Parker saw it for what it was—a life-sized statue of Rosamund herself. Only, it wasn't a statue carved out of stone or marble. The sculptor had created something truly spectacular, a living embodiment of Coronation's patron saint.

Vines wound across the whole figure, weaving in and out to create long legs and a pair of strong shoulders. A head tipped forward ever so slightly, as if to listen. Or maybe to pray. And over all of this, flowers sprang forth in every color, the brilliant display forming a tapestry of life. The purest lilies and softest lilacs. Joyful daffodils and bright peonies. Daisies and azaleas and forsythia. They bloomed across the body of the statue, arranging themselves into a dress fit for a fairy queen.

And finishing it all off—a crown of roses. It was what the girls were all clambering forward for their chance to win. Delicately placed on the statue's head, the blooms alternated between crimson and white.

"It's beautiful," Parker found herself mumbling, her gaze transfixed, not even caring that someone might hear her longing.

She breathed in and smelled the fragrant air again. She imagined she could track the sweet aroma right to that rose crown. And if she somehow won it—if Rosamund chose her as the Rose Duchess—it would mean everything. That she belonged here.

"Here, take my hand," Beth said. "It's about to begin."

And Parker obeyed, not even realizing what she was doing, her eyes still locked on the statue. A girl on her other side moved to take her free hand, and suddenly Parker was part of a chain.

No. A circle. One that wound its way around Rosamund, all fifty girls linked together in an unbroken line with the saint's statue at the center. Beth's hand tugged on Parker's, inviting her to follow, and they started moving, rotating slowly.

The girls stepped together, their motion smooth, as if they were dancing to a song that Parker couldn't hear.

It didn't matter, though. She could keep up. She could stay

in sync. This was nothing compared with a tennis match. She barely broke a sweat. And then, suddenly, there were words. A chant. It bubbled out of the girls' mouths, loud and clear.

Ring around the Rosie,
A pocket full of posies,
Ashes, ashes,
We all fall down.

Parker tripped and almost toppled over as she heard the words. But luckily, Beth's grip kept her on her feet. It kept her circling as the girls continued to chant, starting from the beginning again.

Ring around the Rosie,
A pocket full of posies,
Ashes, ashes,
We all fall down.

She wasn't as shocked the second time through, even though she was still confused. She didn't know the rhyme, but it sounded like something she used to jump rope to as a little girl. She didn't know why they would be singing it here. She didn't know what it had to do with Rosamund or Coronation.

But she kept moving, kept spinning, the spring sun warm

on her face, the scent of flowers sweet in her nose, the chant filling her ears as Beth's hand pulled her along.

Around and around and around they went, until Parker felt like they'd never stop. But she didn't want to. She'd never felt this light, like she could dance on air. Her hair whipped behind her, and she opened her mouth, joining in on the chanting.

Ring around the Rosie,
A pocket full of posies,
Ashes, ashes,
We all fall down.

The circle of girls whirled as one, picking up speed with each revolution. A pleasant warmth stole into Parker's body. She inhaled and her lungs filled up with it.

Ring around the Rosie,

Her tongue grew fuzzy in her mouth. Her limbs started to tingle.

A pocket full of posies,

Her eyes drooped, closing halfway. And then all the way.

Ashes, ashes,

She felt Beth's pulse beating in her palm, pulling her along, keeping her in line as they chanted.

We all fall down.

And then, suddenly, Parker was on her own, tilting forward, losing her balance so quickly it was as if it had been taken from her.

She lifted off her feet and pitched out of control. She toppled out of the circle and through the air, both hands whipping out in front of her, moving to break her fall.

She hit the ground with a *thud*, and all around her the world went quiet. The chanting cut out and the girls stopped moving. A gasp sounded from the crowd. Parker squirmed, too mortified to pick herself up. It was Barf Bag all over again.

Only this was worse. This time she'd embarrassed herself in front of the entire town. Everything was ruined. She'd never be able to live this down.

A hand landed on Parker's shoulder, but she didn't lift her head. She would have buried it in the earth if she could have.

"It looks like Rosamund has made her choice."

Parker looked up then, squinting to make out the headmaster standing there over her, one arm reaching down to touch her shoulder and the other lifted high as he spoke to the crowd.

"Let's all give a cheer for this year's Rose Duchess."

CHAPTER
ELEVEN

Cheers?

Confused, Parker turned her head to stare out at the crowd as they all erupted with applause. Their shouts were deafening, and there were even a few wolf whistles thrown in there. She'd never had anyone cheer for her like this. Not even when she and Dani had won the city championship.

But this couldn't possibly be for her. Not after she'd tripped and fallen in front of everyone.

She'd ruined the game. They all were supposed to fall down together. At least, that was what the song had said. But she was the only one on the ground. She'd fallen too early. She'd made them all stop before the ceremony was done. Before they could choose the winner. Because there was absolutely no way that they'd pick her. She couldn't be their Rose Duchess. She didn't know how to be it. She didn't even know what it *was*. They'd obviously made a mistake.

"Come. Join us." The headmaster's hand moved from Parker's shoulder, and he held it out for her to take. Gingerly, she gripped his fingers and let him pull her to her feet. She took a long moment dusting off her skirt, buying time because she didn't know what to do.

Should she bow and give a pageant wave to the crowd? Did she need to make a speech?

Parker looked at the headmaster and then at his wife. But neither of them made her feel any more relaxed.

It was only when she spotted Beth in the crowd jumping up and down, barely able to contain her excitement, that Parker imagined it could all be real.

"This is Coronation's greatest honor," the headmaster's voice rang out over the crowd. "And I'm delighted to present to you all your next Rose Duchess."

Parker quickly rearranged her face, hoping that she looked the right amount surprised and humbled and elated and grateful. Even though she had no idea what the title entailed, it was obviously a really big deal.

"Your crown," the headmaster said, elongating his free arm so that it stretched out toward the statue of Rosamund. "Shall we?"

He waited. And then, when Parker nodded, he led her forward, bowing before the statue, a grand, sweeping motion that took his whole body to perform. Following his lead,

Parker tipped her chin down and fell into her best curtsy. It seemed like the proper thing to do. And as the crowd grew suddenly quiet around her, she knew she'd made the right choice.

As she rose back to her full height, her eyes took in the statue again. Closer now, she could make out the intricate details, every flower in the prime of its bloom, open wide like delicate mouths gasping for breath. She inhaled and the aromas sent her head spinning. They nearly knocked her off her feet.

But she managed to steady herself, watching as the headmaster reached up and tenderly removed the crown of roses from the statue's head. He held it high for everyone to see, and then turned to Parker, gesturing for her to kneel.

Sinking to one knee, Parker glanced up at the statue of Rosamund, which seemed so much less grand now without the roses ringing its head. Doubt suddenly flooded through her mind once again.

What had she gotten herself into? She didn't deserve this. She couldn't be the town's Rose Duchess. She couldn't be trusted. She'd only let everyone down.

Have faith. You were chosen for a reason.

Parker's heart stopped as the thought popped into her mind. She stared harder at the statue's face.

Had she imagined its lips moving? The way its head had given her an ever-so-slight nod?

"Introducing your Rose Duchess!" The headmaster's announcement startled Parker, snapping her out of her thoughts. She jumped to her feet and only realized that the crown was already on her head when it almost fell off. Steadying it at the last second, she smiled sheepishly out at everyone, their applause the loudest it had been.

"Now let the celebration begin." The headmaster clapped his hands, and it was like he'd broken a spell. Instrumental music started playing out of hidden speakers and everyone turned back to their conversations. They started eating and drinking again like they hadn't just watched a strange children's game played out in front of them.

"Wear the crown well," the headmaster said to Parker before turning and walking away, taking Mrs. York with him.

"You won!" a voice cried.

Parker turned just in time to brace herself for Beth's tackle hug.

"I knew you could do it."

"You aren't mad?" Parker pulled away slowly. She'd been worried about this, about how Beth and the other girls would react. She was new to town and she'd come in here and beaten them, even though she didn't know how or why.

"Of course not," Beth insisted, her voice earnest, letting Parker know that she truly meant it. "Rosamund chose you."

"But why?" This was what Parker really wanted to know. "I tripped. I messed up. I should have gotten last, not first."

"You tripped because she wanted you to."

Parker's brow furrowed.

"She *chose* you, Parker."

Beth's hands shot out and pressed down on Parker's shoulders. She looked her right in the eye and didn't blink.

"You felt her," Beth said. "While we were chanting. I know you did."

It was a wild thing for Beth to suggest. But hadn't she felt something? Parker thought back to that moment right before her fall. But it was blurry. They'd been spinning so fast. She'd felt warm and tingly all over. Her vision had gone fuzzy at the edges. And she'd thought—she'd thought she'd heard something over their chanting.

Someone.

She focused on the memory and tried to recall that voice.

Let go.

Parker's eyes shot open and landed on the statue of Rosamund. Her mouth dropped open. She had to be hearing things. Misremembering. There was absolutely no way—

"She chose you," Beth said more quietly now. Serious.

"I guess she did," Parker murmured. Because what else could she say.

Glancing over Beth's shoulder, she spotted a head of bleached-blond hair bobbing through the back of the crowd, moving against the waves of people. And she suddenly remembered the boy's warning.

Hold on tight. Don't fall down.

His words made sense now. But why hadn't he wanted her to win? Why hadn't he wanted her to become Rose Duchess?

Everyone else was excited for her. They were cheering her on. Lifting her up. While he was trying to drag her down. He'd threatened her and attempted to scare her away.

But it didn't matter what he thought. He was just one person. And clearly a mean and bitter one. Probably jealous of her, too.

Luckily, before Parker could get really worked up, the rest of the girls had crowded in around her and were congratulating her, patting her on the back, peppering her with questions and high fives and hugs. It was all she could do to keep up with them. To soak up their joy. To bathe in that spotlight, the center of attention for the first time in her life.

CHAPTER
TWELVE

Leaves shivered in the night air as a breeze rushed up behind Parker and tousled her skirt. She squinted and stretched her arms out in front of her, but she couldn't see anything past her hands. She had no clue where she was or how she'd gotten there.

The grass crunched underfoot, a soft cushion, as she took a cautious step forward. Slowly, she swung her arms out, jumping as her fingers brushed up against something foreign. Something sharp and dry with thin edges. But then she relaxed a little, her brain catching up to her beating heart, recognizing the papery feel of vegetation. A shrub, maybe. Or ivy.

She took a few more steps, and suddenly the night came to life as if she'd triggered a switch. Hundreds of orbs of light flickered on. They dangled in the air. Pulsing. Humming. Wafting up and down like dandelion fluffs on the wind.

Fireflies, Parker realized. Their soft glow illuminated her surroundings, the walls of a long green tunnel, one that had swallowed her whole.

She blinked and ran her hand over the leaves again, noting how they rose high above her head. Too high for her to climb. So high that they blocked out the stars and moon. And she knew where she must be—the maze in the middle of the school's gardens. But that didn't make sense. She hadn't come in here. The last thing she remembered was climbing into bed. Drifting off to sleep. Her house was a mile from the school. How had she gotten out here?

The breath caught in her throat and her eyes grew wide. She tried to stay calm, but where the air had felt warm before, a sudden chill stole over her, creeping up her arms, clinging to her toes. She had to find her way out of here. And she had to do it now.

Glancing ahead, she saw the hedges raced into a dead end. But turning around, Parker spotted an opening, the path splitting in two. With only one way to go, she set out.

Parker looked left and then right as she reached the end of the row. She had no clue how she was supposed to figure out which way to turn. There weren't any bread crumbs scattered across the ground. No trail to lead her home. But as she was about to resort to eeny meeny miney mo, a firefly careened past her face, grazing her cheek with its tiny wings. It zipped to the left, and Parker turned to watch it go. Then she realized that

95

the rest of the bugs were all heading in the same direction. So she followed.

Left. Right. Left. Straight. Left.

She wandered through the hedge maze, using the fireflies as her guide. With each turn, she felt like she was getting closer to something. But she also felt the temperature drop. She felt eyes watching, like the flowers nestled into the hedges were keeping track of her progress. She kept moving, though, afraid that if she stopped, she'd lose the fireflies, be plunged back into darkness.

Right. Left. Right.

She tried her best to remember the path, to keep her eyes open for any details that would tell her she'd already been there before, that she was walking in circles.

Another left. Then a right. And she stumbled into a clearing.

She glanced around, but there were no ways out except for the path she'd come in through. She'd hit another dead end. Or could she have reached the maze's center?

She spotted a figure up ahead and was relieved to find that she wasn't alone.

"Hello? Can you help me?" Parker's voice echoed in the night air.

But the figure didn't acknowledge her. It didn't move at all. Its feet were rooted firmly in the ground. And as Parker approached, she realized that it wasn't a person at all. It was the statue of Rosamund, the one she'd danced around just that morning.

The saint looked different in the night, her flowers dark and muted. The afternoon had been about hope and celebration, but now Parker could see a different side to Rosamund. Sacrifice and sadness. Survival. What she'd learned from Beth's stories.

Moving closer, Parker studied the statue's features. Even in the dim glow of the fireflies, she could make out its eyes that could have been crying. The mouth curved downward into a frown. The crownless head . . .

Parker's hand lifted to her brow and she felt the circlet of roses there. She worried that she'd taken something from the statue. That she was the reason for its unhappiness. She could give the crown back. Renounce the title of Rose Duchess. An honor like that didn't belong to her.

But Beth had said that Rosamund had chosen her. The headmaster had said it, too.

And then Parker remembered the warmth that had filled her lungs when she'd been announced as the winner. The way her stomach had fluttered as the girls raced in to congratulate her. The cheers from the whole town. All those people looking at her. Happy for her. Proud of her.

She did deserve this. She deserved to be the Rose Duchess. After all, Rosamund had chosen her. The town had, too.

As this new resolve settled over her, Parker looked up into

the statue's closed eyes, surprised to see a teardrop sliding down the saint's cheek.

No. Not a teardrop. Dew. Because statues couldn't cry.

Reaching up, Parker brushed the water droplet away with the back of her hand, and then gasped when the statue's eyes suddenly snapped open.

Parker didn't have time to react. She didn't have a chance to run or fight or scream as the statue's hands flew out and clamped down over her ears. Its mouth opened wide and Parker could count the teeth, two rows of sharp, bloodied thorns.

An inhuman screech cut through the night, and the statue pulled Parker closer, its mouth still open, ready to devour her whole. Parker tried to yank herself loose, but it was no use. The statue was stronger. It had its gnarly hands locked around her neck. She couldn't fight it. She couldn't win. She could only stare into the twisted face of this demon and pray for it to be over quickly.

The teeth came closer and the screech grew louder. Parker closed her eyes. She couldn't face it. She was too scared.

But then, suddenly, she found herself free. She opened her eyes and the statue had disappeared. The screeching had stopped. Parker stood alone in the middle of the clearing, the night pitch-black, the fireflies gone.

A fire flickered to life, blinding Parker with its sudden brightness. She cringed and turned away. But when she looked back, a chill ran down her spine.

Because she wasn't alone. Rosamund stood in front of her, a torch held high in one hand. The flame illuminated the woman's face, dancing across the pale flesh, showing that this wasn't the statue made of leaves and flowers and stems and branches. This was a living and breathing incarnation of the saint.

Wounds dotted Rosamund's forehead, holes that must have come from wearing a crown of roses and piercing thorns. They wept blood, the crimson trails dripping, bringing a hideous color to the woman's cheeks.

Parker's whole body shook, rebelling as she tried to bolt away. Glancing down, though, she saw that her hands were bound together. Her legs were latched to a wooden stake that ran all the way up her back. She tried to wrench herself free again, but her restraints held. She wasn't going anywhere.

Panic rose in Parker's chest. Sweat beaded on her brow. Her heartbeat thundered so loud in her ears that she couldn't hear anything else as the living Rosamund came closer, her torch steady, the flame flickering devilishly. Dangerously.

"No," Parker murmured. "You don't have to do this. You can have the crown back. I don't want it anymore."

A playful smile quirked across Rosamund's lips, but she didn't respond.

"Please." Parker had never felt so desperate in her life.

But Rosamund would not be moved. She would not be persuaded. She kept coming closer until she stood right in front of Parker.

"I'm begging you," Parker whimpered, her forehead drenched in sweat, tears racing down her cheeks. "You don't have to do this."

Rosamund paused then. And Parker prayed that she'd gotten through.

"For long ago the seed was sown."

The saint's voice crackled, parched and paper thin.

"And now it's time to pluck the flowers."

Then, without another word, Rosamund bent low and touched the tip of the torch to the wood stacked at Parker's feet, the pyre catching immediately.

Flames nibbled at Parker's toes. They licked and devoured. They grew high and hungry, grabbing at her legs. Snatching the edge of her skirt. Smoke filled her lungs, but she screamed all the same. She screamed and coughed and screamed some more. She twisted and tried to break free. She fought until she'd worn herself out.

And all the while, Rosamund watched her burn, the saint's expression placid, unfeeling.

"Help—me—" Parker croaked. But Rosamund had no reply for her. No last comfort. Her lips, though, were moving. And when Parker squinted, she could see them whispering something. She held her breath and strained her ears, listening hard. And she was finally able to make out the soft words.

"Ashes to ashes . . . we all fall down."

The fire grew higher, and Rosamund retreated. Pain

scorched through Parker's entire body. It curled up her legs and shot across her bare arms. It latched around her neck and stole her breath. It pulled her under into an inescapable blackness. She screamed one last, desperate cry as she disappeared.

And then, finally, she woke up.

Parker jolted upright in bed, her throat raw and hot, her body bathed in a cold sweat, the sheets underneath her damp with it. Her skin tingled and her forehead burned hot to the touch as her pulse pounded in her throat. Her breaths came shallow and fast. She stumbled out of her bed and grabbed a trash can, heaving into it.

Tears pricked the corners of her eyes as she remembered the nightmare. Remembered the panic that had coursed through her veins and the pain that had shot up her nerves. It'd all felt so real.

But it hadn't been.

She checked her arms and legs. There were no bruises where she'd been bound. No burns from the flames. It'd all been a dream. She was safe.

Her heartbeat slowing, Parker got to her feet. She was still shaking, but she knew it'd pass. She left the trash can on the floor and walked down the hall to the bathroom, flipping on the lights. She ran the faucet, thinking cold water would help with the fever. But when she glanced up into the mirror, she froze. Her eyes bulged. Her shoulders tensed. Her breath caught as she saw her reflection. Saw the streak of blood running down the length of her face, starting in her hairline and descending to the ridge of her chin, marking her cheek like a scar.

Frantically, she fingered the wound, relieved when it smeared and rubbed away. It was only dried blood. Not a cut. She hadn't clawed herself in her sleep. She hadn't let her nightmare terrors take over.

She leaned closer to the mirror and traced the blood up her cheek. She parted her hair and saw the source.

Nothing but a prick really. A thorn stuck into her skin. She hadn't even realized that she was still wearing the rose crown from yesterday's festival. She must have fallen asleep with it on, her pillow pressing the thorn in until it had drawn blood.

Carefully, she pulled it off, remembering her dream. Remembering Rosamund. She stared at the roses, rotating the crown in her hands, counting the blossoms, willing herself to forget what she'd seen. To forget that face with its horrible teeth and its terrifying eyes. To forget the scorching heat as it'd traveled across her body. To forget all about that nightmare version of Rosamund.

CHAPTER
THIRTEEN

Lockers banged up and down the hallway as students packed their textbooks and grabbed their bags to head home. Parker wouldn't be joining them for another couple of hours, though. She had her first tennis practice that afternoon.

Slinging her racket over her shoulder, she turned and jumped when she saw Beth standing right there next to her.

"Sorry, I didn't hear you come up," Parker explained, her hand fluttering near her chest. She was still on edge from last night. From what she'd seen in her nightmare. What she felt like she'd lived. "I'm a bit all over the place today."

And it was true. After she'd cleaned the blood off her face the previous night, she hadn't been able to fall back to sleep. She'd kept hearing things—snaps and cackles and embers popping in the night. And every time she'd gone to close her eyes, that terrible face had appeared in front of her.

Staring off into the distance now, Parker spotted Rosamund's beatific visage staring back at her from a portrait on the wall. The pink, cherubic cheeks were nothing like the pale, horrible ones she'd seen in her nightmare. And Parker wondered how she'd even gotten that image into her head in the first place. How had her brain distorted such a beautiful saint of a woman into that demon who'd set her on fire?

"Bad dreams?"

"Yeah," Parker mumbled, shaking her head as if that would knock her out of her funk. "You could say that."

But it wasn't just in her dreams. She'd seen things while awake, too. At least, she thought she had.

Earlier that morning, when the sun had just started to peek over the horizon, she'd gotten out of bed, finally giving up on trying to get any sleep. She'd gone to her window and leapt back immediately, jarred wide-awake, her heart hammering against her ribs.

Because there'd been someone down in the garden. She'd spotted them plain as day. A figure, cloaked in long purple robes, staring up at her window. She hadn't been able to make out the person's face, but they had been there. Someone had been watching her.

Only, when she'd gathered enough courage to take a second look, the backyard had been empty. No one had been there. Not even a random gardener.

"I guess all of yesterday's excitement got to me." Parker

shrugged, hoping Beth would let it drop. But the reminder only made Beth's smile light up big and bright.

"Our Rose Duchess," she exclaimed. "Long may you reign." And she dipped into a curtsy, bowing low and deep.

"Oh, stop it." Parker swatted at her friend, glancing around to see if anyone was watching them. And as Beth rose back up to her full height, she started giggling, spotting Parker's red cheeks.

"I'm only teasing."

"I know."

Parker tried to calm down, even though it wasn't something that she should be embarrassed by. She just wasn't used to the attention. Her gaze roamed, looking anywhere but at Beth, and she spotted a familiar bleached-blond head hiding half in a doorway, watching her from a distance, his brow furrowed. She hadn't seen him since the festival. Hadn't had a chance to berate him for attacking her. But she still hadn't told Beth about the encounter either.

"Who is that?" Parker asked. But right as Beth turned, the boy disappeared, leaving an empty doorway where he'd been standing.

"Who is who?" Beth asked, confused.

"It's this boy who's been following me around," Parker explained. And then she did her best to describe him. "He's got bleached-blond hair. And he paints his fingernails. He kind of always has a scowl on his face."

"You mean Rider?" Beth asked.

Parker nodded, because that had to be him.

"He's kind of a weirdo," Beth said. And it surprised Parker a little. This had to be the first time she'd ever heard Beth talk down about someone. "I mean, he doesn't really fit in. I don't think he has any friends. Did he try to talk to you?"

"No."

Parker didn't know why she'd lied. She wasn't protecting him or anything. But hearing Beth talk about him like that, it reminded her of something Callie might have said behind Parker's back.

"Don't worry about him," Beth went on. "His sister died last year in some kind of awful accident. And I think he's still really torn up about it."

So he'd lost his sister. Not that it was an excuse for his behavior. But Parker understood him a little more now. She didn't have a sister, but she didn't know what she'd do if someone close to her died. Someone like Dani.

The name sliced through her and she realized she hadn't thought of Dani in what felt like weeks. But the idea of Dani being taken away from her was too much to bear. Even though she still hadn't spoken to her, Parker could still reach out if she wanted. They might not be friends anymore, but at least she was still alive. There was hope that maybe one day they could be close again.

"Do you want to walk down to the courts together?" Beth

suggested, wrapping her arm through Parker's and pulling her back to the present. "Do you have everything?"

Parker patted her racket and nodded. She had her clothes and shoes in her backpack. She could change in the locker room.

"Let's go."

Parker gave in to Beth's pull, following her down the hallway.

Before she'd gone completely, though, she took one last glance over her shoulder. But the boy—Rider—hadn't reappeared.

"I can't believe we both made the team."

Parker tuned back in to Beth's gushing. If there was one thing she'd learned about her new friend, it was that the girl could talk. About anything.

"This is going to be so much fun," Beth jabbered on. "Do you think the coach will let us play doubles together? We did so well in the tryout. We're a natural team."

Parker nodded, knowing that Beth would roll right along without her. Which worked for her because she hated having to fill the quiet. Hated the pressure of saying the right thing. She was happy to follow. It kept her out of trouble.

"Where are you all rushing off to?" she heard a voice say. And Parker felt Beth jerk her around before she even registered who it was.

"Why are you bothering us?" Beth scoffed, rolling her eyes.

Turning, she saw Brady closing his locker, his shirt untucked and his tie loose in that casual way that was meant to look haphazard but was definitely intentional.

"It's our first day of tennis practice." Beth rolled her eyes at her older brother. "You're going to make us late."

"I just wanted to wish you luck," Brady replied, unbothered by Beth. "To you and to Parker."

Parker was surprised he'd remembered her name. And a little confused. Brady had ignored her since that morning on her driveway. And even then, he'd only said like two words to her. She didn't feel comfortable around him.

And it wasn't just that he'd ditched her on that first day of school. He had red flags waving all around him. He was a jerk. She knew the type. He thought he owned the school. Thought he was too cool to even acknowledge someone like her.

"Thanks," Parker mumbled, because it was the polite thing to do, even if she didn't like him.

"I'm sure you two will be great," Brady said. Parker wondered if Beth felt the same awkwardness thick in the air. "My mom mentioned that you played at your old school?"

Parker froze up, thrown that Mrs. York would talk about her. That she'd tell Brady and he'd actually remember it. It was strange to imagine her name coming up in conversation over their dinner table. Why would they care about her? About her past? The things she was good at?

"Oh, she's the best on the team," Beth jumped in when Parker didn't reply. "You'll have to skip your precious lacrosse practice sometime to come watch us play. Then you can see for yourself."

A pause stretched between them, and Parker felt Brady sizing her up, the corner of his mouth twitching slightly, playfully.

"I'll have to do that." He nodded as if making a mental note, marking it off in his social calendar.

"Have fun at practice, little sister." And then, with a tip of his head, he was gone, disappearing down the hallway, probably heading off to that lacrosse practice Beth had mentioned.

"Just ignore him," Beth said, rolling her eyes again.

But before Parker could internalize how weird that whole exchange had been, they were off running again, racing through the hallways and out the back door.

As they hurtled down the sloping lawn, though, her thoughts caught up to her. Had Brady been flirting with her? No. That was impossible. She was a freshman. And new to town. She wasn't cool enough for that.

But maybe she was.

Now that she thought about it, that parting nod had definitely felt like something more. Like if he'd just bent a fraction lower, he would have been bowing to her.

"Beth?" Parker asked, making the girl pull up short in the middle of their dash to practice. "How big a deal is being named Rose Duchess?"

"The biggest."

That didn't really help explain it, so Parker pressed on.

"So is it kind of like winning prom queen or something?"

"Oh." Beth sucked in an excited breath, barely able to contain herself. "It's way better than that. You're royalty now."

Parker's cheeks burned red at the way Beth said it. At the reverence she gave the title.

"But it can't be that big a deal, right?"

"You'll see." Beth nodded knowingly. "Your life is about to change."

Parker didn't like the way that sounded. It had an almost ominous ring coming out of Beth's mouth.

But then again, was change that bad? This was an entirely different experience than her old school. People seemed to like her here. They noticed her. Celebrated her. But a boy like Brady crushing on her? That was too far. It was impossible. Not even a crown could get someone like him to like someone like her.

Or could it?

And did she even want that?

Parker shook her head and tried to clear her thoughts. It was all so complicated. She had enough to worry about right now. Rider. What she'd seen in her nightmare. Her paranoia. She had to make sense of everything going on around her.

110

CHAPTER
FOURTEEN

Parker crept through the rows of flowers, unsure if she was allowed to be there. It was five o'clock. The school day was long over, but she hadn't been able to help herself. She had to get another look. Otherwise, she didn't know if she'd be able to sleep that night.

After maneuvering around a particularly stumpy shrub, Parker paused and tried to orient herself. The hedge maze couldn't be that hard to find. It must take up a decent amount of space.

Confident in her plan, Parker got back to walking, heading in a direction she thought was north, away from the tennis courts where she'd just wrapped up her first practice.

She thought it'd gone well. The girls had all been friendly and welcomed her to the team without any cold shoulders or initiations. And when the coach had put her with Beth for doubles, the girl had let out a high-pitched squeal and danced across the court. After running some drills, they'd ended the afternoon by playing a practice set against a pair of seniors, which they'd won.

Parker had to admit that they worked well together, Beth responding to her calls, listening and covering the court. It hadn't been as seamless as playing with Dani, but it had been good enough. And the way Beth had lit up when they'd won—Parker could get used to that. She could live on that appreciation and excitement for weeks.

She felt kind of bad now for the way she'd ditched Beth at the end of practice, cutting around the corner when she wasn't looking. But it would have been too hard to explain why she needed to sneak into the gardens. Why she had to check out the hedge maze. She didn't need Beth thinking there was something wrong with her. That she couldn't handle a little nightmare. A silly bad dream—

Suddenly, something snatched the collar of Parker's shirt and yanked her backward, ripping her out of her thoughts. She freaked as she fell and hit the ground, her arms and legs spinning like a turtle trapped on its back. Her eyes darted around the garden, searching for the security guard who must have caught her.

But no one was there. And Parker quickly realized that it wasn't a hand that had pulled her backward. It was a branch, snagging on the handle of her tennis racket, which was sticking straight up out of her backpack.

She felt like an idiot. Her cheeks burned hot with embarrassment, and she was glad that no one was there to witness her ungraceful panic. The way she'd been floored by a tree.

Picking herself up, she brushed off her hands and realized that she'd arrived. The maze was right there in front of her, impossible to miss. She took a few steps forward, until she came right up to the base of the hedge and suddenly felt so much smaller.

She craned her neck and deduced that the hedge walls had to be at least eight feet high. They towered over her and the rest of the garden, blocking out the view so that all Parker saw was a leafy expanse of green, like an ocean or the sky. Infinite.

Turning, she followed the maze to the right, skirting the edge, waiting for an entrance to open up. Which it did after a couple of minutes.

Parker hesitated, taking in the corridor in front of her. She saw that a tunnel shot through the green foliage. It was just like in her dream.

But she was here to prove that it wasn't real. That she'd imagined everything. She'd come all this way. She couldn't turn back now.

She plunged forward, not leaving any more time to hesitate, letting the maze engulf her.

She moved through the hedgerows, her fingers trailing

along the wall, the leaves as dry and paper thin as they'd been in her nightmare. It looked different in the daylight. But also, different because this was real. This wasn't something that she'd dreamed up.

Still, a part of her worried that if she slowed down, if she stopped to think, her fears would catch up to her. Her nightmare would come true.

So she kept moving, turning this way and then that, not keeping track of where she'd been or where she was going. Not thinking of how she'd get back out once she'd seen whatever it was that she was here to find. She didn't know what exactly she was looking for. And maybe it wasn't that she needed to find something—but that she needed to prove that something didn't exist.

Turning down a new row, Parker startled.

An image flashed through her head. A memory.

The fire.

Smoke.

Someone screaming.

Her breath caught in her throat and she gasped, realizing it was her own scream choking her.

She blinked and found herself back in the garden. But she could still smell the smoke. She could still hear the crack of wood as it splintered under the intense heat. And someone was suddenly there in front of her, waiting at the end of the path. Just like in her backyard that morning.

Only, Parker realized, they weren't moving. They weren't coming after her.

Cautiously, she took a few steps closer, and she saw that it wasn't a person at all. It was a statue, just like the one they'd danced around at the Bloom Festival. But this wasn't Rosamund. It was someone different. A girl with dark hair and a dress made of violets.

Parker didn't know who it was supposed to be. If it was another representation of Rosamund or a different saint altogether. It was beautiful, though. A work of art. From a distance, it could have passed for a real girl.

But as Parker got closer, the details showed through. The willowy fingers and carved-out eyes. The way the statue's feet dug into the earth, anchored and immovable.

As Parker took a closer look, examining the sculpture like she hadn't been able to with Rosamund's, a chill tickled her body. Something compelled her to reach out and touch it, to feel the bark and flower petals. To see if the violet dress moved like the fabric it was meant to mimic. It called out to her, and she felt that if she closed her eyes, she might be able to hear it. To understand what it was trying to tell her. She leaned in, and another vision flashed in front of her.

Teeth bared. A cackle. Voices chanting. More fire. Fire that Parker could feel the heat from. Fire that licked at her toes. That climbed up her legs. That threatened to devour her whole.

She blinked and pulled away, her heart racing.

Had the statue been reaching out to her like that before? Had it moved? Was that the same sad expression it'd had on its face before? Or was she reading too much into it? Was she being paranoid?

Parker took a step back, giving the statue one last look before hurrying along the path. She'd always thought that porcelain dolls were creepy, but human-sized statues were so much worse.

Getting to the end of the row, Parker turned the corner, happy to have distance between her and that thing. But as soon as the relief hit her, she froze. A cold dread dropped into her stomach.

She couldn't have gotten turned around, could she? Had she somehow gone in a circle?

She steadied herself against the maze wall, feeling suddenly nauseous. Feeling the nightmare tapping at her thoughts again as she peered at the figure standing at the end of the row, waiting for her like she'd never left.

But no. This wasn't the same statue. It had a different-color gown—marigold yellow—and spiky pine cones sticking out of its head for hair.

It was another girl. Another saint or nymph or whatever. Maybe a sister of Rosamund. Beautiful but creepy.

Parker didn't stop to take a closer look as she moved into the next row. Where she came across yet another statue. And then another in the row after that.

These wore lily-white and peony-pink gowns. And Parker was starting to wonder if they had a purpose. Could they be leading to somewhere? In her dream, the fireflies had guided her to the center of the maze. Maybe these maidens would help point her to an exit.

She kept going, ducking through the leafy corridors, brushing past the figures until she reached an opening in the maze that was guarded by two women, twins in matching carnation gowns, only one was red and one was white. They flanked the entrance, their hands held up in prayer, their heads bowed. And in those poses, Parker knew that she'd found what they'd all been pointing her toward. What she had come into the maze to find in the first place. She steadied herself and took a step forward, a small, circular clearing opening up around her. Just like in her dream.

And there in the middle of it all, the statue of Rosamund.

Parker stuttered backward, her shoulders colliding with the hedges, the foliage crunching under her weight.

The sound broke her concentration. It took her out of whatever spell the gardens had cast on her. All that twisting and turning and the uncertainty of where she was going, it'd done a real number on her. But now she could see that there was nothing to be afraid of. And wasn't that why she'd wanted to explore this in the first place?

Yes, Rosamund standing there in the center of it all might have been eerily similar to Parker's nightmare. But that could be a coincidence. She hadn't dreamed about the maiden statues. And she hadn't pictured that white rose either. The one that was growing right out of the ground at Rosamund's feet. It was so beautiful, so purely white, that Parker had a hard time believing she hadn't dreamed it.

The Rose of York. The oldest flower in the garden.

Parker remembered the story Beth had told her. About how the settlers had brought it over with them from England. About how they'd planted it here in the center of the garden. About how Rosamund had appeared and saved them all.

And now that Parker took a good look, she noticed how Rosamund was positioned over the rose. How she was protecting it, her arms stretched out wide to shield it from the elements.

Parker took a couple of steps closer, her gaze transfixed on the rose. How had it survived for centuries? Was that even possible? Or was it only a nice story the townspeople liked to tell?

The tips of her fingers prickled as she extended her hand, reaching for the white petals, wanting to brush their glossy texture.

Not yet.

The voice crackled through the air, startling Parker.

Something sank its teeth into her wrist, refusing to let go.

Panicking, Parker's eyes shot down and she saw a pair of twig nubs pressing into her flesh. They felt like bones, sharp and brittle. And when Parker looked up to see her attacker, she nearly fainted. Everything in her wanted to cry out for help, but something kept her frozen.

Rosamund.

The real one. Her eyes burning orbs, the same haunting ones Parker had seen in her nightmare. Living and breathing and moving in front of her. Her blond hair flowing behind her in a tangled mane. Her skin, ashen flesh. The blood dripping down her cheeks from those puncture wounds in her forehead.

Don't worry. You'll have your chance to burn soon enough.

The smell of smoke filled Parker's nostrils. It coated the back of her throat. She coughed and tried to get rid of it. But now the smoke had mixed with the perfume of the flowers. With the White Rose of York right there under her nose.

The scent was sweet and sickly. Like what Parker imagined was the scent of burning flesh.

She kept coughing as she squirmed, frantic and terrified. Because this wasn't a dream. She couldn't just wake up and everything would be fine. If she didn't get out of here, that was it. The end.

She planted her feet on the ground. She pulled with every muscle in her body. And then, with a sickening snap, she finally managed to break free.

She didn't waste a second. She tore out of there, fleeing blindly, racing by the statues she'd passed on the way in, each one a blur of gnarled hands and hollow eyes. A different color of the rainbow that bled into the next.

She turned down rows and rushed through dense green tunnels. She didn't stop. She didn't dare look back. She didn't think about how she was going to get out of there. She just had to put as much distance between herself and that nightmare as she could.

She felt tears wetting her cheeks, making the world even blurrier. But she didn't blink. She was too afraid of what she'd see if she closed her eyes. She shouldn't have come in here. Her dream had been a premonition. Why hadn't she listened?

Another figure suddenly appeared at the end of the row, and Parker didn't know what to do. She couldn't escape them. There was nowhere else to go. Everything in this maze looked exactly the same. She'd gotten turned around and she had no idea how to get out.

"Leave me alone!" she shrieked, her arms flying out, fighting the best that she could as she collided with the figure. As hands grasped her wrists again and pulled her down.

"Look at me, Parker," a voice called through her delirium. "It's going to be okay. I know the way out."

And as the fight left her, Parker blinked her tears away and saw a head of bleached-blond hair hovering over her. Rider.

CHAPTER
FIFTEEN

She collapsed into him, burying her face in his shoulder, her tears and snot rubbing into his shirt.

"What are you doing here?" she murmured, her voice muffled, sounding far away even to her own ears.

"I was following you."

Parker's heart stopped. Everything that Rider had done came back to her. She jerked away from him, examining his face. But there was no apology there. Just pure stalker vibes.

She was suddenly aware of how alone they were. Just the two of them trapped in the maze. He'd already grabbed her once. She didn't want to give him the chance to do it again. Or worse.

Carefully, she backed away, keeping her eyes on the boy. Watching for any sudden movements or lunges in her direction. Her fingers reached back and grabbed the handle of her tennis racket, ready to unsheathe it, swing it at his head if she had to.

"I'm not going to hurt you," Rider spat out, as if the idea of it was distasteful.

"Like I'm going to believe that," Parker threw back. "You've threatened me twice. And attacked me once. Why would I trust you?"

"I can get us out of here."

"You know the way out?"

Parker's hands shook as she weighed her options. She knew she couldn't trust him. But that thing was still in here. That demonic Rosamund and all her sisters.

"Yeah," Rider assured her, his tone still brisk, as if she'd insulted him with the question. "I've been mapping it out for months. Sneaking in when I could. Doing a section at a time."

"Show me."

Rider sighed, but then he rummaged in his pocket and pulled out a piece of paper, holding it up for her to see.

He really had mapped it out. Parker's eyes darted across the page, taking in all the lines zigging this way and zagging that. It was a complicated series of narrow passageways and dead ends that branched out in all directions before disappearing into the center of the bull's-eye, a blank, uncharted zone.

"I haven't gotten to the center yet," Rider huffed, as if he'd heard her question and taken it as a criticism. "But it's enough to get us out."

Then he turned the paper in his hands, using it like he might a compass, and took off down the row.

"Are you coming?"

There was nothing else she could do. She didn't have any other options. But she kept her distance. And kept her hand on her tennis racket. She wasn't afraid to whack him if he tried anything.

They didn't speak as they walked, Rider's focus trained on his map, on navigating them out of there. Parker was fine with that, though. She needed time to think. Time to figure out what exactly had happened back there.

Her wrist still throbbed, and there were the pricks in her arm where the statue, or whatever it was, had grabbed her. So that, at least, had been real. But even with that proof, it sounded impossible. Rosamund couldn't actually have attacked her. Could she?

Maybe her eyes were playing tricks on her. Maybe the sleepless nights had caught up to her. Had she drunk enough water during practice? Was she dehydrated? Was she seeing things?

But the cuts were there. She hadn't imagined that. Could it have been her own fault? Could she have snagged herself on a branch or caught her wrist in a rosebush?

It all seemed plausible now. She couldn't trust her own memory. Couldn't believe what she'd thought she'd seen. Not when it didn't make any sense. Not when it was impossible.

"So what happened back there?" Rider's question broke through Parker's thoughts. "You were pretty upset. You seemed . . . terrified."

It felt like he was leading her toward something. An admission that she didn't want to make. But he couldn't have guessed what she'd seen. What she *thought* she'd seen.

"I got lost," Parker muttered. "And scared. I don't do well in tight spaces."

That was all she planned on giving him. At least until he gave her something in return.

"Why were you following me?" And then, because she wanted to make it clear: "Why have you been harassing me? What did you mean when you said that it wasn't safe for me here?"

Rider grew cagey all of a sudden, his eyes darting everywhere but at her.

"Well?" Parker demanded an answer, her fist tightening around her racket handle. "After everything you've done to me, you owe me an explanation."

Rider's familiar grimace returned, and Parker gave up hope of getting anywhere with him. But then, he cracked, an answer dribbling out from the side of his clenched jaw.

"The Rose Duchess ceremony was only the beginning. They chose you on purpose. It's all part of their plan. They're coming for you. Just like they came for my sister."

"Your sister?"

It slipped out before Parker could stop herself. But she had an idea of where he was going with it. Hadn't Beth mentioned his sister had died in an accident? That he was in denial about what had really happened? That he still carried that grief around with him?

"What happened to your sister?"

Parker asked the question delicately. But it still froze him in place. His shoulders arched and she almost ran right into him before she could stop herself. He stood there quietly for more than a couple of seconds until Parker thought she'd have to pinch him to wake him up. But then, finally, he spoke.

"She died."

Parker had known this, but hearing it still broke her heart. As awful as he'd been to her, no one deserved to have something like that happen to them.

"How did she die?"

Parker whispered the question and gently placed her hand on his back, wanting to comfort him. She knew it must be hard for him to talk about, but she needed to know what Rider thought had happened. What made him think that the Rose Duchess had something to do with it. She needed to be able to make sense of it all. Otherwise, why was he following her around? Why was he threatening her? Why did he want her to leave so badly?

Rider looked at her and she held his gaze, willing him to tell her the truth. But after a moment, he only shook his head, his shoulders slumping as he turned back around and set off walking.

"You wouldn't believe me."

"I might."

And Parker wished she'd been firmer. That she could have convinced him. But he was done talking about his sister. And before Parker could pester him about it more, they'd turned a corner and found themselves looking out into the main clearing.

"We made it," Rider said. He tilted his head forward and Parker could see the entrance opening up into the rest of the gardens.

"You did it," she cheered, even though it came out as half-hearted. She clapped him on the shoulder and tried to sound grateful. "You're a genius."

He shrugged her hand off, but he still seemed pleased with himself. And relieved.

"Let's get out of here."

The two ran the last stretch, sprinting out of that green-walled prison. And even though the air wasn't any different here, it tasted sweeter to Parker. Like she'd been holding her breath for the last hour and could finally let it go. She inhaled and smelled the flowers, the subtle bouquet of everything from the gardens mixing. Next to her, Rider sneezed, wiping his nose on his sleeve, his eyes watering, too.

"Allergies," he explained as he dug into his pocket and

pulled out a small vial. He popped the top and shook out a round white capsule. Then he swallowed it down in one gulp.

"The pollen here kills me," he explained as he sniffled some more.

He seemed better outside of the maze. But he still had a sad look about him. His whole face drooped—eyes, lips, brow—and Parker wondered if it was permanent. She couldn't even begin to guess how heavy a thing like grief was. Or how long Rider would have to carry it around for.

She felt sorry. She'd seen a different side to him. And he had come to her rescue, even if the only reason he'd been in the maze was because he was following her. She wasn't about to forgive him for everything he'd done, but she could at least be nice to him. She knew what it was like to be an outsider. She knew how hard that label was to carry.

"About your sister—" Parker started, but Rider cut her off.

"Just trust me. You need to get out of here. Leave. Coronation isn't safe. Not for you."

He hadn't understood. She hadn't wanted to ask how his sister had died. She'd wanted to offer her condolences. To tell him that she was sorry.

"What are you doing out here?"

Rider jumped as a voice came up from behind them. Parker could see the panic on his face, the way his hands shook. But it was only Sister Florence, her navy robes billowing behind her. The old woman couldn't hurt them. Not even with the long garden shears she had tucked under one of her arms.

"Sorry, Sister Florence," Parker replied, trying her best to sound innocent, even while Rider stood next to her, sweat beading on his forehead, looking like he'd just robbed a convenience store.

"Were you in the hedge maze?"

"Of course not," Parker assured the woman, even though she could tell that the sister didn't believe her.

"Well . . ." Sister Florence stretched the word out as if she were deciding what to say next. "You should watch out. Especially in there. If you get turned around or lost . . ."

She cut off then, glancing around, and left it at that. Whatever it was she'd thought to say, Parker could only guess at it. But Parker didn't need any more reasons to steer clear of the maze. She wasn't going anywhere near it. Not anymore. She still didn't know what to believe. The more she thought about it, the more unreal it felt, like a memory fading until it was gone.

Statues coming to life? Trying to burn her at the stake?

It was ludicrous. Like something out of a horror movie.

"You all better get going," Sister Florence insisted, shooing them along with the handles of her shears. "It's getting late and your parents will be looking for you."

Parker didn't argue as she pulled Rider along with her. They walked quickly through the garden, not looking back.

But as they were about to pass out of sight, she took one last glance over her shoulder, catching Sister Florence standing there by herself. The woman had turned toward the maze, her shoulders squared, her garden shears held out in front of her, almost as if she were preparing for battle. And it made Parker wonder what exactly the woman would need those blades to protect herself against.

CHAPTER
SIXTEEN

"Come in."

The headmaster's voice rang through the door, and Parker, having no other option, carefully pushed it open.

"Ah, Parker. Please, join me."

Parker hovered in the door for another second and then took a step into the headmaster's office, taking the empty chair across from him.

"You asked to see me?" she mumbled. She'd never been called to the principal's office and didn't know what to do with herself. "I'm not in any trouble, am I?"

Parker thought about how she'd snuck into the gardens earlier that week. About how she'd gotten lost in the hedge maze. No one had told her that it was off-limits, but she hadn't seen any students going down there. Other than Rider. And she was pretty sure he didn't have a problem with breaking the rules.

"Trouble?" the headmaster chuckled. "Of course not."

"Then why did you call me here?"

"I wanted to check up on you. Make sure you're settling in."

When Parker didn't respond, the headmaster plowed ahead.

"You're new here, and I know that can be hard. But you've been getting top marks on all your assignments. And Beth tells me that you joined the tennis team with her. You're doubles partners?"

"Yeah."

This was the one question Parker felt like she could answer. Though it was strange again, to hear that the Yorks were discussing her. But why wouldn't they? Beth was basically her best friend now. And hadn't Parker talked about the girl to her parents?

"That's good," the headmaster said, folding his fingers together and leaning back in his chair. "So, do you have anything on your mind? Any questions for me?"

Parker didn't want to seem rude, so she let her eyes slip from the headmaster's, let them wander around the room while she counted down the seconds, hoping to get out of here without actually having to talk.

The headmaster had a lot of stuff in his office, books and vases and photographs. Brady, Beth, and Mrs. York all stared out at her from several different angles, creeping her out just a little bit. On a back table, there was some kind of scientific equipment set up. Maybe an experiment in progress? The headmaster had a microscope and a few test tubes. An eyedropper and a sharp-looking scalpel. And there was a flower, although it wasn't any that Parker recognized. The stem had been dissected so that its core was exposed. The petals had been peeled back to get a clearer look at its insides, the stamen and anthers and pistol.

"My latest experiment," the headmaster said, following her gaze. "I'm a bit of a biology nerd. In my free time I like to test out new splices and grafts. See what I can get to grow."

"Cool," Parker mumbled, trying to sound as uninterested as possible.

"Any questions at all?" the headmaster prodded. "Anything you need to get off your chest? You can trust me. I want what's best for every one of my students."

Parker didn't believe him. It wasn't like she could tell him about her nightmares. About what she'd seen in that maze—the figure that had been following her around all week. Standing outside her window in the dead of night. Tucked behind the trees during tennis practice. Watching and waiting. For what, Parker had no clue.

No one else had seen it, not even when Parker tried to point it out.

It was always there and then gone. And Parker wondered if the nightmares were truly getting to her. If the lack of sleep was making her delusional.

She closed her eyes for a second to rest, and when she opened them, Rosamund was staring back at her.

Not the real Rosamund, at least. It was only a picture of her. Because just like in every other room at the school, the headmaster had her on his office wall.

"Who exactly is Rosamund?"

Parker didn't know why she'd asked the question, but it was something that had been on her mind. And if she knew a little bit more about the saint, then maybe she could put these nightmares to rest.

"Rosamund is our savior," the headmaster said simply. "She's a guiding light for every citizen of Coronation. A beacon of hope during even the longest winter."

"But where did she come from?" Parker didn't have time for platitudes.

"Well, we brought her with us. When we left England."

Parker squinted, not following, and the headmaster settled back into his chair. This was apparently a topic he enjoyed talking about.

"You see, our ancestors—the founders of Coronation— were exiles. They were forced to leave their home and cross to the New World. A treacherous journey that there would be no going back from. So they packed their most important belongings and got on a boat.

"But the voyage was harder than they'd imagined. Storms blew them off course and wrecked their supplies.

They were soon starving and hopeless. But there was one item they held on to. One thing that was too valuable for them to lose."

"What was it?" Parker whispered, finding herself drawn into the story and the headmaster's telling of it. If nothing else, he was good at that.

"A single white rose. The only one they'd been able to bring with them."

Parker sucked in a breath, remembering what she'd seen in the middle of the hedge maze. The way Rosamund had been shielding it with her body.

"They cared for that rose on their long voyage," the headmaster explained. "They nurtured it and sacrificed their own supplies to keep it watered. To keep it alive. And when their ship finally came ashore, they planted it in the soil, the last symbol of their home, standing as a reminder of who they were."

Parker nodded. She understood what it felt like to move. To leave everything behind. But it wasn't objects that made her feel at home. It was people. It was her parents. It was Dani.

"It was that rose," the headmaster went on, winding his way to the end of the story, "that the settlers went to in their time of need. When their supplies ran low before winter was over. When they had nothing. When death was certain.

"They prayed to that rose, and God listened. Rosamund sprang from the petals, pale as the winter snow, and she brought them back to life. She showed them how to live. She saved them."

The headmaster waved his hands with a flourish and then cupped them as if he were holding a precious rosebud in his palms.

"But what about the Rose Duchess?" Parker asked, afraid to hear the answer. "Who is she?"

"She's Rosamund's helper, of course," the headmaster replied with a slight chuckle. "A symbol in her own right. A stand-in for Rosamund. But no less important."

Parker bit her nail. It sounded like a lot of responsibility. A lot of pressure. She didn't know if she could handle it.

"Don't worry," the headmaster assured her. "Rosamund chose you for a reason. You're more than capable. I know it."

A squeamishness settled over Parker. She wished she had the same amount of faith in herself. She kind of wished she hadn't been named Rose Duchess at all. It was a lot of expectation.

"Now," the headmaster said, clapping his hands together and getting back to business. "We're having a get-together at our house on Sunday. A few other kids from school will be there. Beth, too. It's a kind of youth group. I hope you can join us."

"Sure."

The yes had come out of her mouth before she'd had time to really think about it.

"Well, we look forward to seeing you."

And then, with a flick of the wrist, he dismissed her, letting her head back to class wondering what, exactly, she had just signed herself up for.

CHAPTER
SEVENTEEN

The Yorks' living room was packed. It was more than just a "few other kids" who had shown up. When the headmaster had invited her to come, he hadn't exactly explained what they were supposed to be doing. She'd assumed it was going to be a study group or something. And at the very least, she knew Beth would be there. Maybe someone would tutor them. Or they'd work on their homework together. She'd brought her backpack just in case. But now she wasn't so sure.

"Want one?" Beth asked as she plopped down next to Parker on the couch. She held a cookie out in one hand, but Parker shook her head.

"Is there coffee?" she asked instead. And when Beth motioned behind her to the kitchen, she got to her feet.

"Don't worry," Beth said as she took a bite of the cookie. "I'll save your seat."

"I'll be right back."

Parker shuffled away, weaving through the other students, keeping her head up as she scanned the crowd, looking for a familiar bleached-blond head.

She'd hoped he'd be there today. It was kind of the main reason she'd shown up. After everything that had happened in the maze earlier that week, she still needed to talk to him. She still needed answers.

She'd looked for him at school every day after that, but hadn't spotted him once. And now that it was the weekend, she didn't know where to begin to look for him. She didn't have his home address or know where he liked to hang out. She didn't even have a friend of his that she could ask. She'd never seen him talking to anybody.

He truly was a loner. At least at her old school she'd always had Dani. But Rider—Rider had no one.

Standing in the kitchen, Parker took her time pouring a cup of coffee. She carefully streamed in the milk and sugar, swirling it all together with a tiny teaspoon. She kept her eyes peeled on the door, keeping tabs on all the latecomers straggling in.

None of them was Rider, though. And she realized that he wasn't going to come. But then, that shouldn't have surprised her. This—even though she didn't know exactly what to make of it—was definitely not his scene.

"Parker."

She jumped as she heard someone calling her name, some

of her coffee spilling out of its mug and scorching her knuckles. She shook her hand up and down as she blew on the skin, and she spotted Beth leaning through the kitchen doorway, beckoning for her to hurry.

"It's about to start."

Grabbing a napkin off the counter, Parker scurried forward as fast as she could without spilling her coffee, meeting Beth back in the living room just as the headmaster made his grand entrance.

"Welcome," his voice rang out, and everyone took their seats, a hush falling over the room as they turned to listen. "It's so good to see you all this afternoon."

The headmaster stood in the entryway, looking strangely comfortable in a navy pullover and khakis. He'd even styled his hair differently, letting his gray curls ruffle naturally around his ears.

Behind him, Brady suddenly appeared, the last to arrive even though they were meeting at his house. He came into the room with his usual cool confidence, like he'd just tumbled down the stairs from his bedroom. He had on a York Rosarium sweatshirt and a pair of athletic shorts. It wasn't his usual prep school getup, but it suited him all the same. As he passed into the room to take a seat, his eyes met Parker's, lingering, and her heart hiccuped. But luckily, before she could redden and completely embarrass herself, the headmaster cleared his throat and continued.

"We have quite the turnout for today's meeting. Mostly familiar faces . . . but a couple of new ones as well."

Parker found herself staring at her lap. She'd been in Coronation for over three weeks now and was tired of being the new girl. However, the headmaster didn't push the issue as he plunged right into his talk.

"Today I want to tell you a story."

As the headmaster unfurled his words, he meandered through the crowd, pacing among the boys and girls spread out on the floor and in the chairs. Unlike in their chapel meetings, everyone watched him with the same devout attention, giving the room a subdued energy as they all hung on his every word. Parker could understand that, though. Hadn't she been pulled under his spell, too? When he'd told her about Rosamund in his office? There was a magnetism to his voice. Something that you couldn't help but be drawn in by.

"Now, who can tell me about the fishes and the loaves?"

The headmaster paused in the center of the room.

"Parker? Do you know the story?"

She panicked, squirming on the couch. How was she supposed to know? Why was he setting her up for failure by calling on her?

"It's one of Rosamund's parables, isn't it?" Beth jumped in. And Parker silently thanked her for the save. She imagined it must be awkward for Beth, being as he was her dad. But it made Parker all the more grateful.

"That's correct."

The headmaster turned back to the room as he picked up his lecture.

"A town faced with famine must make a hard choice. There weren't enough fish for everyone to survive and the harvest was too small to bake enough bread to sustain them all. So what do they do? What would you do?"

The headmaster went around the room, calling on people at random. Some offered up serious answers on rationing, saying that they would forage to supplement what they already had. And others threw out harsher ideas. Things like hoarding and resource guarding. Every person for themselves. As the two sides got going, the arguments grew more spirited, until Parker couldn't hear much of anything over everyone's shouting.

"While I appreciate the debate," the headmaster said, waving them all down as he chuckled, "this is exactly why Rosamund had to step in. She saw that no one was willing to make the tough decision. The only one that would actually save them."

He waited then, giving them all one last chance at the riddle.

"They could give up their food?"

Parker didn't know why she'd spoken. The story was new to her, but her old coach used to tell a story just like it. She knew what it meant to be on a team. What it meant to work together. That the whole was more important than the individual player. That sacrifices were required.

141

"Very smart."

The gleam in the headmaster's eye was almost spooky.

"Sacrifice," he exclaimed. "That's what the parable is about. Someone has to be willing to give up their share so that there's more for everyone else.

"But Rosamund was cleverer than that. She knew that taking fish from one man to feed another would only go so far. If they wanted to truly solve their problem—to make sure that no one went hungry—then the fish needed to go to feeding the future. Instead of eating the man's sacrificed portion, they'd mash it up and plant it in the soil. They'd fertilize the field so that the next year's harvest was bigger and better. So that they'd have plenty of bread to go around. So that everyone would eat and be happy and full."

The headmaster wrapped up his sermon to a roomful of nodding heads. But Parker couldn't stop wondering what had happened to the man who'd given up his portion. Did he starve? Had he made it through the winter? What was the price of his sacrifice?

The questions tugged in the back of her brain, but she didn't feel like asking them. She didn't want to set off another debate. She could take it at face value. Stories like this were easier that way.

"I think you all have heard enough from me for one afternoon," the headmaster joked. "But stay and hang out. Relax. There are plenty of snacks. You all know where the fridge is."

A couple of woots floated through the room and everyone started to stir, getting up from the floor and stretching their legs. They milled around, chatting and high-fiving each other. Getting more food. But Parker stayed put on the couch, her eyes watching the headmaster. Watching him watching them.

She didn't know why his sermons made her uncomfortable. They didn't seem to bother anyone else. But there was something about them. They appeared so harmless on the surface, but when she dug into them, there was always more there. A darker streak. She couldn't be the only one who saw it, could she?

She didn't know what to think. None of it mattered anyway. She wasn't going to become a Sower—or whatever they called themselves—any time soon. She just had to put up with hearing the teachings at school.

And they were harmless. They really were.

But if that was true, then why did she have such a hard time convincing herself of it?

CHAPTER
EIGHTEEN

Parker was lost. The Yorks' home felt like being back in the hedge maze. There were so many crisscrossing hallways and she'd already counted like fifty identical doors, all of them shut tight, looking like they had something to hide. When she'd set out from the living room, she'd only wanted to find the bathroom. But now that she was away from everyone, she kind of wanted to explore. To snoop, just a little bit. She knew virtually nothing about the Yorks, and yet they seemed to know so much about her.

Tiptoeing down a long hallway, Parker paused to examine the wallpaper. It looked old and ornate. Dark red flowers bloomed across the expanse, with forest-green leaves filling the space between. Thin lines of gold filigree spiraled through it all, and Parker couldn't help but trace the vines, following them down the hallway, stopping short when she came to a painting hanging on the wall.

Turning, she glanced behind her. She'd thought she'd heard a creak. The house was huge, and she'd wandered pretty far back. Focusing back on the painting, Parker let her eyes take it all in. Judging by everyone's curly wigs and ruffled petticoats and oversized kerchiefs, it had to be from a very long time ago. From colonial America or something, with their George and Martha Washington vibes.

Taking a step closer, she zeroed in on the people's faces, the ten or so of them arranged around the parlor, lounging, standing, eating, drinking, laughing, and toasting. It had to be a celebration of some kind. A wedding or a birthday perhaps.

Parker leaned in closer to look for more clues, and she started as a face popped out at her. One she knew. Only, she hadn't recognized him at first, not with the white wig covering most of his head. But now as she looked at the painting harder, there was no denying the resemblance. No getting around how shockingly similar the man looked to the headmaster. They had the same flinty eyes and stern smile. The same stiff posture.

It couldn't actually be him, of course. But it had to be one of his ancestors. It seemed like a lot of people in town could trace their lineage back to Coronation's founders. And as Parker had the thought, she spotted another familiar face.

Mrs. York, her hair much longer and spilling down her back in blond waves. Her dress a deep rose red to match the wine in her glass. She stood in the center of the painting, everyone's attention focused on her, her drink held high as she toasted them all.

For some reason, Parker really wanted to know what they were celebrating. What could have been so important that they'd commissioned a painting of it? It wasn't like taking a photograph. These things would have cost money and time. She glanced to either side of the frame, hoping she'd find a placard that could give her a clue, but she didn't see anything.

"It's called *The Crowning of Mildred Price*."

Parker's whole body tensed, and she nearly knocked the painting off the wall and onto the floor as Brady sidled up next to her.

"She was the first Rose Duchess," he explained, all calm and cool, like he hadn't just caught her sneaking around his house.

Parker gritted her teeth, waiting for him to yell at her or kick her out. He'd been nice to her once, but she still had her reservations. She hadn't forgotten his flakiness. Hadn't forgotten the way he walked around the school and town like he owned them. Like he was better than everyone else.

But as Parker braced herself, she realized that he wasn't going to tell her off. In fact, he didn't seem mad at all. He was acting like he'd invited her there. Like he was giving her the grand tour.

"That's Mildred."

Parker was surprised when Brady pointed to the corner of the painting. She'd assumed the title subject would be in the middle, but in this case, Mildred was on the edge, a beautiful young woman in a delicate purple dress, the skirts sheer and light, making her look like she would fly away if a breeze blew in through the room. And in her hair, unmistakable to Parker now even though she hadn't noticed it at first, was a circlet of red and white petals—a crown that matched the one Parker had back in her room.

Parker's breath caught in her lungs.

"Who are they?" she finally asked.

"They're the founders of Coronation," Brady replied. "Celebrating the spring after surviving that first winter."

"Are they your ancestors?" Parker turned to Brady, realizing it was a silly question. But he had a smile on his face. A laugh on the tip of his tongue.

"You noticed the similarities?"

Parker nodded, still wary, but warming up to him with each passing second.

"It's kind of hard to miss," she said slyly, meaning it as a joke.

"My family's been here forever." Brady dipped his head, almost as if he were embarrassed by the fact. And Parker marveled that he could feel that way. That he had an ounce of modesty in his body. "My mom and dad can both trace their roots back to the first settlers."

"I guess that makes you royalty around here."

"And yet, you're the one with the crown." Brady's lips quirked up. But something in that statement made Parker frown. "What's on your mind?" Brady's tone had turned serious.

He nudged her, which made Parker waver. There were so many confusing thoughts all mixed up in her head. But did she really want to talk to him about it?

"What does it mean?" she eventually blurted. "To be the Rose Duchess?"

She'd been asking everyone—Beth, Rider, the headmaster—and they'd all given her different answers.

"It means . . ." Brady drew his answer out as he thought about it. "It means that you're the most popular girl in school."

Parker batted him away.

"I was being serious."

"So was I."

Brady feigned offense before continuing. "But also, I guess, the Rose Duchess stands for hope."

"Hope?"

Parker's scrutiny seemed to stump Brady, and they both stared at the painting, their unspoken thoughts thickening the air between them.

"Do you know the full history of Coronation?" Brady eventually asked. "Of why the settlers came over in the first place?"

Parker shook her head. Beth and the headmaster had told her parts of the story, but they hadn't said why the settlers had needed to come over in the first place. Just that they'd had to leave everything behind.

"They were cast out of Europe for their beliefs," Brady explained. "They came here to escape persecution. Risked traveling across the ocean to build a place where they could live freely and plant new roots."

The Sowers. Now their name made sense.

But it wasn't like their teachings were dangerous. At least, not that Parker had seen. They actually weren't that different from a lot of other religious groups. They were centered in kindness and community. In what was good for the whole, outweighing the needs of the few.

"The Rose Duchess is meant to symbolize that new beginning," Brady went on. "The sacrifices the settlers made to start all over again."

And Parker could see where he took after his dad. How he had a way with words and capturing a person's attention. It was a side to him that she hadn't seen before. It surprised her, but she liked it. He had a deeper level to him.

"But she's also meant to represent the outcasts," he continued. "That's why we choose the first who falls. During the ceremony. To show that every single person matters. It's an honor. Really. It means you're special."

Parker couldn't tell if he was flirting with her or if she only hoped that he was. Either way, she couldn't look at him. Couldn't let him see how flustered he'd made her.

Did he really think that? That she was special?

"Are you okay?" Brady's hand grazed Parker's elbow, and she tried to wave him off. But she felt the need to say something. To make him understand.

"I didn't fit in at my old school," Parker said. Then she paused, losing herself in her thoughts as she remembered what it had been like before. How lonely she'd felt. Even with Dani. "But here, everything is different. I feel like I matter. Like I actually belong somewhere."

And saying it out loud made her realize just how much she needed that. She craved it. So much so that she didn't care if it made her sound desperate. She didn't care if it gave her nightmares. She didn't care that she hadn't slept a full night in over a week and that there might be something lurking in the school's hedge maze. She didn't care because, in that moment, it all seemed worth it.

Brady smiled at her in a way that told her he understood. "Should we head back?" he asked. And Parker liked him a little more because he'd let her vulnerability drop.

"I could really go for a cookie," she said. "And another cup of coffee."

"After you." Brady bowed low, gesturing for Parker to take the lead, and she made sure to bump into him as she passed, knocking him off balance just a little, causing him to chuckle as he stumbled after her.

CHAPTER

NINETEEN

The porch swing creaked underneath Parker as she swayed in the early-evening air. She used her tiptoes to keep herself rocking while she sipped on a glass of lemonade, the cool droplets of condensation slipping down and chilling her fingers. She was lost in her thoughts, staring into the rosebushes that buffeted the porch, their blooms on full display, peppering the air with their sweet perfume. An undercurrent of smoke seeped through the aroma, and Parker wrinkled her nose, her hand squeezing the glass of lemonade tighter.

She stared harder at the flowers. But something changed. Their blossoms turned into eyes. The crimson petals blurred, weeping blood. A scream welled up from somewhere far away, growing louder and closer until it was right behind her, filling her ears, coming from her own throat.

She startled and nearly fell onto the porch. The swing

rocked precariously underneath her, and it took her another moment to steady herself. She looked back at the rosebush, but the eyes were gone. The screaming had stopped.

Had she fallen asleep?

She shook her head and tried to wake up. Tried to forget the nightmares. To forget what she'd seen in the hedge maze.

No. What she *thought* she'd seen.

Because it still seemed impossible. She'd been dehydrated and exhausted. She'd felt disoriented and panicked after getting lost. Her imagination had spooked her. It made her see things that weren't there.

She closed her eyes and the images flashed in front of her again. The fire. The roses. The statue of Rosamund bearing down on her. Snatching at her wrists. Pinning her in place. Burning her at the stake.

It'd seemed so real. A waking nightmare to go with all her sleeping ones.

That was why she'd been setting her alarm to go off every half hour, to wake her up in the middle of the night. She had to stop the nightmares before they got out of hand. Before they pulled her too far under. She hadn't had a full night's sleep since the Bloom Festival. Since being named Rose Duchess. Which was over a week ago.

She rubbed at her eyes and pinched her arm. She didn't know what was bothering her, but enough googling told her that nightmares were a symptom of stress. The move. Or maybe the way she'd lost Dani.

She pulled out her phone and scrolled through her social media feed, stopping as Dani's face popped up on the screen. The girl was standing arm in arm with Callie, the two of them holding their rackets high in victory. The caption read: *New partner, same winning ways.*

So Dani hadn't gotten suspended from the team. She hadn't lost her scholarship.

A part of Parker was happy. Relieved. But she still felt a stab in her gut. A tightening in her chest. Her fingers hovered over the screen. And then, before she could think better of it, she tapped out a comment and posted it.

I knew you could do it.

It would be up to Dani to decipher what Parker meant.

I knew you could win. Or, I knew you would move on without me.

Parker wasn't sure of the answer herself. Why wouldn't she expect Dani to find a new partner? She had. And Parker couldn't be mad at Dani when she was the one who'd left. When she was the one who'd ruined things.

"Are you doing okay out here?" Parker's mom asked, poking her head out the front door. "Need anything? More lemonade?"

Parker shook her head and gave her mom a smile that must not have masked her tiredness very well. Her mom pushed the rest of the way through the door and walked out onto the porch, leaning against the rail as she fixed her daughter with a concerned look.

"How have you been holding up? I've been so busy with everything that I haven't stopped to ask you. Do you like it here? I know it's different. I know you're probably missing—"

"It's great here, Mom," Parker insisted. "Really."

"Then why do you seem so sad?"

"I'm not."

Parker sat up straight on the porch swing. She couldn't let her mom think that. They'd come here for a shot at a fresh start. At repairing what had been broken with their family. And despite her sleepless nights, everything was working. Her dad had a great new job. Her parents weren't fighting anymore. They had this huge house to live in. She was making friends at school and finally felt like she fit in.

"I guess I've just been a little tired lately," Parker explained, hoping that would be enough to calm her mom's worries.

"Is it the schoolwork? Is it harder here? Are they asking you to do too much?"

It wasn't. But Parker didn't want to tell her mom about her bad dreams, so she nodded.

"I can talk with your teachers. See if they can help you out since you transferred in mid-year."

"It's fine," Parker assured her mom. "I'm catching up. And if I need help, Beth said she'd tutor me."

She hadn't, but Parker knew that the girl would if she asked.

"She's your new doubles partner, right?"

Parker nodded.

"Well, she sounds like a good friend. I'm glad you two hit it off. You must be missing Dani."

An uncomfortable quiet fell between them as Parker dropped her eyes to the boards at her feet. If she looked up now, it'd all be over.

"Have you heard from her?" And even though it sounded like an innocent enough question, Parker could tell her mom had picked up on something.

"Yeah," she squeaked out. "Actually, I was just messaging with her."

"That's so good to hear."

Her mom smiled, and it made Parker feel terrible for lying to her. But what else could she do?

"You two were so close. You always looked out for each other. Seeing you girls split up—that was the worst part of this move. It's why I almost convinced your dad not to take the job."

"You did?"

"Why do you sound so surprised?"

"I guess—" Parker fumbled for what to say. "I thought we needed this."

Parker's mom paused. She pushed herself off the rail and

155

came over to sit next to Parker. She leaned in and pressed her forehead against her daughter's, holding her close.

"Were your dad and I fighting? Sure. Did he need a job? Yes. Could we use the change? Definitely."

Parker couldn't remember her mom ever talking to her like this. So openly and honestly. It kind of scared her. It made her see her parents in a new light.

"But," Parker's mom went on, pulling back and turning Parker's head so that they were looking directly at each other. "Just like with friends, families fight. They go through rough patches. It gets hard. It feels bleak. But then, usually, they figure it out."

Parker swallowed down the tears building at the back of her throat.

"Your dad and I want what's best for you." She pushed a piece of hair behind Parker's ear. "So if something isn't working—if something doesn't feel right—then you let us know. This move doesn't have to be permanent. Not if you're not happy."

"I am, though."

And Parker squeezed her mom's hand to make sure she knew how much she meant it.

"I promise."

Her mom held her gaze. "But you'll let me know if things change?"

Parker paused, and then nodded. However, in the back of

her head, she told herself that, no matter what, she wouldn't say anything. Things were good now. But even if that changed, she couldn't risk going back.

"You want to wash up for dinner?" Parker's mom asked as she stood up. "Your dad's on his way home. He had to work late. There was an emergency at the Rosarium."

Parker perked up.

"Don't worry. It was just some kids pulling a prank. Tagging the building again."

Her mom dug in her pocket and took out her phone. She pulled up a photo and showed Parker.

"Your dad sent it to me."

Parker scooted forward and took a look at the image, her gaze sweeping over the brilliant green beetles that were crawling up the side of the building, taking big bites out of the wall as they climbed. It was Rider's handiwork. Parker knew that now. But she still didn't know what the little bugs meant. She'd looked for him again at school that day, but he'd run the other way every time she'd spotted him in the hallway. Apparently he'd been busy, though. Which could have been why he was avoiding her.

She knew his secret—that he was responsible for the graffiti all over town. Maybe he was afraid she'd tell on him. It'd be a good way to get back at him for everything he'd done. But he had gotten her out of that maze. She didn't owe him anything, but she didn't want to get him into trouble. At least, not until she talked to him. Not until she made him explain.

"I'm sure your dad will catch them soon," Parker's mom said, taking her phone back as she took a step toward the front door.

"I'll be right there," Parker said, getting up from the porch swing as her mom disappeared inside.

But instead of following her, Parker turned and looked back at the rosebushes. The flowers smoldered in the waning light, as brilliant as ever. And Parker couldn't help but reach out and hold her palms over them. Brush the silky petals.

She pulled back as a sudden pain cut through her. And for a second, she thought she'd been burned. But it was only a thorn snagged on her finger.

Carefully, she pulled the prick out and watched as a drop of blood bubbled up and grew on the surface of her skin. She was transfixed by it, unable to turn away even as a chill crept up her spine. She saw Rosamund's face reflected there in its shiny surface, the blood dripping from the woman's forehead, staining her too-pale face. She saw a fire in the demon's eyes. She saw—

A rustling jerked Parker's attention away, and she dropped her hand.

Her head flicked to the side. She had to squint to see, marveling at how dark it had gotten, how suddenly the sun had disappeared. But the figure watching her was unmistakable even though it'd changed the color of its cloak. It was a brilliant orange tonight, standing out like a beacon in the dark. It was too far away for Parker to make out its face, but she could see its red lips. The crown of roses nestled on its head.

"What do you want from me?" Parker cried out, low enough that her mother wouldn't hear.

When the figure didn't move or even acknowledge her, Parker jumped off the porch, her fists balled at her sides.

"Leave me alone," she declared in a hoarse whisper.

And then, when the figure still hadn't moved, she sprinted forward, eyes watering, the night turning blurry, her exhaustion fueling her, her desperation separating her from the fear, making it so that she could ignore it.

But when she got to the spot where the figure had been standing, it was suddenly gone, leaving Parker there alone in the night, her chest heaving, her heart racing, and her hands shaking uncontrollably, not knowing if someone had really been there or if she had hallucinated the whole thing.

CHAPTER
TWENTY

Parker's head tipped forward, her eyes fluttering shut, the clock on the wall ticking like a metronome, lulling her under with its steadiness. Her breathing slowed and the teacher's words blurred together, fading into the background. Her neck craned in on itself and her forehead grazed the desk.

But before she could give in to her desperate need to sleep, she snapped back up, stretching her eyelids wide, the air drying out her pupils, making her eyes even more bloodshot than they'd been that morning. She reached down and snapped the rubber band around her wrist, hoping the sharp pinch would keep her up.

And it did, for a couple of minutes. But as the scratching of pencils filled the room, Parker started drifting again. Her head dipped. Her eyes closed and opened and closed and opened. She snapped the rubber band, but she could barely feel the pain anymore. She could barely hold on.

"Parker?"

She blinked and looked up at the teacher who'd just called her name.

"Well, do you know the answer? Did you even do the reading last night?"

Parker fumbled with her book, flipping through the pages, glancing at her notes, hoping that something would pop into her head. She had done the homework, but she couldn't remember any of it now. She couldn't make out any of the words in front of her. Couldn't even remember what class she was in.

"I—" Parker stuttered, looking up from her desk, catching every eye in the room trained on her, waiting for her to fail. "I don't know. Can you repeat—"

"You're going to have to work harder if you want to keep up," the teacher pronounced, his voice gravely disappointed.

Parker tried to explain. She tried to tell him that she'd done the reading. But her tongue had grown heavy in her mouth. A fog had seeped into her mind. She could barely keep her eyes open. She felt anxious and sick to her stomach and raised her hand to ask to go to the bathroom, but then, suddenly, she couldn't move her arms.

She glanced down at her desk and her stomach really did heave. A dribble of vomit shot up into the back of her mouth. Her heart started knocking against her rib cage. She blinked and tried to reset. She tried to see through the hallucination.

Through the vines that had sprouted from her desk and wrapped their thick tendrils around her wrists.

But they wouldn't go away. And as Parker tried to pull herself free, she could only scream as thorns ripped through her skin, shredding her flesh, spilling her blood.

"Help me," Parker whimpered, turning to her classmates. But they all just stood there, staring at her, their eyes big and empty.

"No one can save you," a voice hissed. And Parker gasped as she turned and saw Rosamund standing at the front of the room.

"Get away from me," Parker shouted, her feet scrabbling against the floor.

But her desk didn't budge. It was rooted to the floor, the vines thickening, overtaking the wood and her chair, wrapping around Parker until she couldn't move at all, until she could only wriggle.

Suddenly, the room pitched into darkness. Everything went silent. Parker strained to hear, but she thought she was alone. She tried to calm down. She tried to think. She could get out of this. She could escape.

She winced at the sound of a match scraping against a surface. Parker had to swallow her scream as a torch flickered to life, illuminating Rosamund standing there in front of her. Their eyes were level, and Parker realized she was on her feet. Only, her wrists were still bound, and someone had looped a rope around her chest and legs, pinning her to the spot.

Parker felt hot liquid dripping down her cheeks. But it was thicker than tears. Redder. She couldn't wipe it away, but she knew what it was. Could feel the pain of the thorns circling her head, digging in, giving her wounds that matched Rosamund's.

"You can have it back," Parker whimpered, wishing she could lift the crown off her head and throw it at Rosamund's feet. "I don't want it anymore."

But Rosamund didn't listen. She merely lowered her torch and let the flames leap to Parker's pyre, engulfing her.

"Help me!" Parker shrieked. "Someone. Anyone. Help me."

But now that the fire had grown, she could see her classmates gathered in a circle around her. Yet no one seemed to hear her pleas. They only watched, their faces unmoving as the flames climbed. As they flickered and spat and fed. As they took bites out of Parker's flesh.

"Please."

She tried one last time, her voice strained, her throat raw and cracked.

But no one moved. And soon, Parker couldn't see anything but the fire. Couldn't feel anything but the scorching pain.

CHAPTER
TWENTY-ONE

The sound of the bell ringing jolted Parker awake, and she jerked out of her chair and onto the floor, landing in a pile of twisted limbs and tousled hair.

"I'm fine," she assured everyone, her cheeks flushing with embarrassment because they'd all stopped to stare. But at least they could see her. They hadn't forgotten her. Not like in her nightmare.

As everyone started to filter out of the room, Parker picked herself up slowly, keeping her head down so as not to make awkward eye contact with anyone. She waited a few beats longer for the last stragglers to clear the room, and then she turned to go herself. But she stopped almost immediately, a strangled yelp dying in her throat.

One of the many portraits of Rosamund was there, staring at her. The beautiful young lady with blond hair and smooth skin. But her eyes were just as haunting. They pierced Parker with their stare. They bored into her just like they had in her nightmare.

She shivered at the memory, growing anxious with how inescapable Rosamund had become. They had her face hanging on almost every wall in the school, surveying the hallways and classrooms and chapel. Parker couldn't get away from her. She could feel those painted eyes crawling across her back, keeping track of her every move, and she had to get out. Out of the room and out of the building.

Parker pushed through the corridors, ducking between her classmates and teachers, not slowing down for anyone. She didn't stop at her locker or ask for a hall pass. She just booked it, weaving in and out and around until finally she burst through the back doors of the school and felt the grass underneath her feet. Then, finally, she could stop and breathe. She could release the tension that had built in her shoulders. She could think about her master plan.

She exhaled and willed herself to calm down. She'd had a plan when she'd arrived at school that morning, but she couldn't go back in there now. Not that it really mattered, though, since her strategy had failed spectacularly so far. She'd had her eye out for Rider all week, and every time she'd spotted him in the hallways or after chapel, he'd turned and run the other way. He'd avoided her, and she didn't know why. But she needed to talk to him. She needed him to explain. He was the only person who she thought could give her answers. But she'd only ever actually gotten the chance to talk to him when he'd rescued her from the hedge maze.

Parker's jaw tightened as an idea came to her. She didn't like it, but she was desperate. And it might be the only way to get him alone.

She glanced over her shoulder but didn't see him. He'd been stalking her before, though, and so she hoped that he was out there following her still. So with a sense that she was making a terrible mistake, Parker set off down the sloping lawn, heading for the last place she wanted to go.

It didn't take her long to make the trip, to walk beneath the gardens' gates. But this time she did it with dread prickling the back of her neck. She felt sick to her stomach as she drifted along the paths, hoping that Rider would appear sooner rather than later. That she could get his attention without having to go into the maze.

Unease clung to her, its invisible spiderweb threads pulling her back, warning her to listen to her gut. She knew this was a mistake. But she promised herself she wouldn't go in. Not after last time. Not for anything. This was just bait. A way to lure Rider out. And then they could talk.

When the hedges rose up in front of her, Parker stopped. In the bright afternoon sunshine, they didn't look threatening. But she'd been inside. She'd seen things.

So she waited, willing Rider to appear in front of her as

she stood there in the middle of the same clearing where she'd been crowned Rose Duchess. She spun around in a circle, searching for him. She would have shouted if she hadn't worried that someone else would hear and come running.

What was he doing? She was starting to get annoyed. He'd been following her before, but now when she actually needed him, he was nowhere to be found. She couldn't keep going like this. Couldn't keep seeing things. Couldn't keep not sleeping. She'd already started to crack, and she didn't know how much longer she could go until she broke apart completely.

She stubbed her toe in the dirt and kicked a rock across the grass, watching as it dribbled into the maze. Then an idea struck her. What if he was already inside?

He hadn't finished mapping it out yet. But he wouldn't dare explore it all on his own, would he? What if he got lost? What if he ran into trouble? She couldn't get answers out of him if he hurt himself. If something in there got him.

Parker took a step toward the entrance, balancing on her toes, gravity threatening to tip her forward and plunge her into the maze. She searched the ground for a piece of string or a trail of bread crumbs, anything that Rider might have used to find his way back out. But the path was clear. There wasn't even the shadow of a footprint dinting the grass.

Which meant he probably wasn't in there. He didn't need her help.

But what if he was? And what if he did?

Parker wavered, unsure of what to do. He'd come in after her. But then, he'd seen her go in. She couldn't risk looking for him based on a feeling.

"I thought I told you to be careful around that maze."

Parker pulled back and shot a look down the row, spotting Sister Florence approaching, holding the large pair of garden shears in one hand as she carried her trusty bucket in the other.

"I'm not going in there," Parker assured her, feeling her head clear as she took another step away from the entrance. She couldn't believe she'd entertained the idea of going after Rider.

"You don't want to get lost."

Sister Florence punctuated each word with a shake of her shears, and Parker had to lean back to avoid getting a sharp blade to the face.

"What are you working on today?" Parker asked politely, nodding toward the sister's bucket.

"Fertilizer. And pest control."

"Can I help?" Parker asked, needing something to fill the time while she waited for Rider. And to be honest, she was kind of curious, and relieved to have someone else there with her.

"This way," the old woman said, and Parker moved to follow her.

They walked over a couple of rows and then the woman planted her bucket in the ground. She buried the shears and began digging through the bottom of the bucket, taking out handfuls of fine powder that she spread over the roots of the nearest bushes.

"What's that?" Parker asked, poking her head closer. "It looks kind of like ash."

She made to dip her hands inside to feel it for herself, but Sister Florence stopped her.

"Fertilizer. But you don't want to get any on your clothes. It'll never come out. And it stinks."

Now that she mentioned it, Parker realized that it did reek. Almost like dead fish. Which reminded her of the headmaster's parable.

"Is it like the fish and the loaves?"

Parker was proud that she'd remembered, and she was rewarded when Sister Florence gave her a crinkled smile.

"Yes. Only, this isn't dead fish. We've evolved since those days. Found something that works even better."

Parker wanted to get her hands dirty, too, but she held back, watching Sister Florence work. The woman scattered another handful of fertilizer over the ground and used her fingers to massage it into the soil, then she wiped her hands and started examining leaves. She picked up one and then another. Then finally on her third leaf she called Parker over.

"See this?"

Sister Florence held the leaf between her fingers, pulling it close but making sure she was gentle with it so that it wouldn't snap off the stem. Parker crouched to get closer. It looked kind of like a lace doily. Or a paper snowflake. The middle was all chopped up with holes punched out in random patterns, the veins of the leaf the only thing left intact.

"They've been skeletonized," Sister Florence said.

Parker didn't like the sound of that. But she saw how the word fit. Squinting, she could see the form of a skull on the leaf—the holes that would be eye sockets, the split that made a mouth. It was fitting. And morbid.

"What did that?" Parker asked.

"Japanese beetles. The rose's natural predator."

She'd never heard of those before, but she figured they must be nasty.

"They can't do too much damage on their own," Sister Florence continued. "But when they team up, they'll devour a whole plant in an afternoon."

"How do you stop them?"

"You have to find them and pick them off." Sister Florence rummaged in her bucket again and pulled out a jar. "Can you open this for me?"

She handed it to Parker, who unscrewed the lid.

"Is it poison?" Parker took a cautious sniff, but it didn't smell lethal.

"Just soap and water. They can't swim in it."

170

Sister Florence took the mixture and began flipping leaves over, examining their backs until—

"Got you."

Her fingers flew forward and she plucked two bugs off the leaf. She quickly dropped them into the jar and gave it a good shake. After a few seconds she held it up to Parker, the pests floating on the top of the water, no longer moving.

Parker gasped and covered her mouth.

"It doesn't hurt," Sister Florence said. "I promise. If we let them run wild, they'd eat the entire garden. There'd be no more roses. No more Coronation."

"It's not that." Parker stuttered after a few seconds. "I've just—I've got to get going."

And without any further explanation, she stood up and took off.

But as she retreated, she couldn't stop thinking. Couldn't stop worrying. Because the insecticide wasn't what had bothered her. It was the bugs themselves, their familiar coppery-green wings glinting in the sunlight. She finally knew what Rider had been drawing. And she might have figured out why.

CHAPTER
TWENTY-TWO

A natural predator.

Parker swatted at the back of her neck as if the bugs were crawling across her right then, preparing to bite holes out of her skin. To skeletonize her.

Did that mean that Rider was trying to eliminate the Rosarium? Rosamund? The Rose Duchess? Her?

He'd adopted the beetles as a symbol. He'd left his graffiti all over town. He'd broken into the Yorks' offices. He'd threatened her. And even attacked her. She'd seen what he was capable of.

Maybe he *did* want to hurt her. Maybe he wanted to hurt every single person in Coronation. She'd seen his anger firsthand. How it was twined with his grief. Something like that could smolder into a flame. Could burn down an entire town if it went unchecked.

But then, why had he helped her when she'd gotten lost in the maze?

It didn't make any sense. It was too much to think about. Too confusing. But the symbol had to mean something. It had to have been chosen for a reason. Rider had warned her to leave. Would he really go that far to get rid of her?

Footsteps padded through the grass behind her, and Parker turned. But before she could process it, Rider was standing next to her, huffing a little bit, looking like he'd run to catch up to her.

"Hold up," he panted. "Where are you going in such a hurry?"

Parker jumped back, her thoughts spinning, her guard up. She'd been trying to talk to him for so long, but suddenly the thought of being alone with him frightened her.

"What are you doing out here?" Parker asked, trying to keep her voice from breaking. She eyed his fingers, the white rose he had cupped in his hand.

"And why do you have that?"

"It's food." Rider twirled the flower around as if it was obvious.

"For what?" Parker asked hesitantly. And then she watched as Rider fished underneath his shirt and pulled out a glass mason jar that was almost identical to Sister Florence's.

Only, Rider's wasn't filled with water. And the beetles inside were very much still alive.

"Are those . . . ?"

"Japanese beetles," Rider affirmed.

And then, working fast, he unscrewed the lid and dropped the white rose in, closing the jar back up before any of his jade pets could escape.

"It's not quite a swarm," he explained, which was an understatement. He only had about twenty-five beetles. He'd need thousands to get to plague level. "But I'm working on it. Training them up."

He lifted the jar so that Parker could get a better look. Inside, the beetles had already started in on their lunch, working their way up the stem, maneuvering around the sharp thorns to get to the leaves.

"Why?" Parker wondered out loud as she watched a beetle take a bite out of the rose.

She shivered as she imagined them crawling along her arms. How long would it take for them to devour her? How much would it hurt?

"Why are you trying to destroy the Rose Duchess?" Parker was amazed at how calm she sounded. At how her voice didn't waver. But her hands gave her away. They shook with each word, so she stuffed them into her pockets and tried to keep it together.

She was so tired. Tired of running but not knowing what from. Tired of having questions without any answers. Tired of feeling this all-consuming paranoia. Of not knowing what was real and what was imagined. The nightmares and Rosamund and Rider—it all bled into one giant, monstrous mess. If she didn't get some kind of clarity soon, she was going to have a nervous breakdown. She was going to explode.

"Tell me," Parker demanded. And the command in her voice surprised even her. She hadn't known she could be so assertive. She'd only ever had this kind of confidence on the tennis court, when she was smashing winning volleys at the net.

"It's not you," Rider finally got out, stumbling over the words. "I promise you. It's Rosamund. She's who I'm trying to stop."

"Rosamund?"

Parker's voice broke, and she realized what she'd been searching for.

Validation. It wasn't all in her head. She wasn't going mad.

Relief spilled through her. Because Rider had seen Rosamund, too. Parker wasn't alone.

"She's poisoning this town," Rider said, his words coming faster now. "She's got everyone in a trance. She's using the roses. The scent—it gets in your head. It makes you see things. Makes you do things. Makes you forget. She's got everyone brainwashed."

The momentary relief Parker had felt started to slip away with every word out of Rider's mouth. It was like she had a flower and he was plucking a petal off with each wild theory that flew out of his mouth. Pretty soon, she'd have nothing left.

Sure, she'd seen Rosamund in her dreams and in the maze. But a scent that could control people? Roses that could make a person forget?

Rider must have seen the doubt in Parker's expression. "You don't believe me. It's true. I'm not making this up."

"Well . . ." Parker cast around for something she could use. A hole in his story. "Why hasn't the magic worked on you?"

"My allergies," Rider said. "I'm so stuffed up, I can barely smell anything."

And this, though it still sounded far-fetched, made Parker consider what he was saying.

"I think the headmaster is involved, too. And the rest of the Sowers. Or they could be under her spell. I don't know yet. I'm still trying to piece it all together."

He rushed to get it all out, and Parker found herself actually listening, worrying about what his story could mean for her. For her family. For Beth.

But what was she even thinking, entertaining Rider's wild notions? It was something straight out of a horror movie, and Parker assumed that if she went home and looked it up, she'd find a similar story floating around somewhere on the internet.

"What do the beetles stand for?" she asked, getting back to her original question.

"It's the symbol of the resistance."

"The resistance?"

Was Rider working with other people? Had he convinced someone else of his story?

"Well . . ." He stretched it out, buying for time. "It's just me right now."

"And how have you been resisting?"

Parker hoped it was limited to the graffiti. She couldn't imagine Rider's skinny self getting up to more trouble than that.

"I've been breaking into their offices. Sabotaging their plans."

So he was behind it all. He was the person her dad had been hired to find. The one causing all the trouble.

"What plans?"

She still wasn't sure if she could believe him. But she was intrigued by it all.

"They lure their victims here," Rider explained, his shoulders falling, relieved that he finally had someone willing to listen to him. "It's how they work. You. My sister. And who knows how many girls before that."

"So their entire scheme hinges on whether or not they can convince people to move to Coronation?" Parker raised an eyebrow. It didn't seem like a foolproof plan at all.

"We only moved here last year," Rider went on, talking faster now, as if he were on the clock. "When some great-aunt on my mom's side died and left us her house. But the thing is, my mom didn't know that this great-aunt even existed. We still moved, because the house was big and paid for and the school had a really good music program for my sister. Morgan played the flute."

He threw in the last part and Parker could tell how much he missed her. How much he still mourned her loss.

"Then, a few weeks after we got here, Morgan was named Rose Duchess—just like you—and everything spiraled out of control."

Quiet fell between them as Parker thought about everything that had happened to her. Had Morgan gone through the same things? The nightmares and the paranoia? That feeling that someone was watching her?

"What happened to her?" Parker wasn't sure if she wanted to know, but she couldn't not ask.

"I don't—I don't really know." Rider started to get choked up. "But it wasn't an accident. They never found her body. Something happened to her. People don't just disappear. They're not here one day and gone the next."

"What do you mean, gone?" Parker asked, unsure if she wanted to know the answer. But she needed to hear it. Needed all the details. "Did your parents look into it? Did they talk to the police? Was there a search party or something?"

"No," Rider scoffed. "They believed the lie. The head-master and his wife came over one morning and sat us all down.

They had a police officer with them, but they told the story themselves. They told us that Morgan had been out with friends and that they'd been playing flashlight tag or something. They said that she hadn't watched where she was going. That she'd slipped and fallen off one of the cliffs. That they hadn't found her body and it must have washed out to sea. It was no one's fault. Just a terrible accident."

Rider broke down then, a sob climbing its way up his throat.

"Did they say anything else?" Parker asked gently. "Did they say who she was with?"

"No," Rider replied, shaking his head, tears flying off his cheeks. "They gave their condolences and the headmaster said a prayer, but that was it. And I could tell something was off. It was the way he looked at me and my parents. He fed us the story of how she'd died and convinced them to accept it and not ask any more questions."

Rider's hands had balled up into fists and they shook at his sides.

"I knew it was a lie. But I could tell he wanted us to believe it. The way he talked—it was almost like he was planting the memory in our heads, sowing the seed of it. So I pretended. I went along with it. And my parents did, too. Only, they never snapped out of it. They actually bought it as the truth."

"But—" Parker cast around for the right words to say. The

story couldn't end like that. There had to be something. More leads or—

"You must know who her friends were," Parker insisted. "You saw who she hung out with at school. We can find them. See if they remember anything from that night."

"But I don't know."

Rider buried his head in his hands, tearing at his hair.

"I was going through some stuff last year. I came out right before the move and it was just—bad timing. I couldn't handle it all. And I was a terrible brother. I didn't know what was going on in Morgan's life. I didn't know if she was dating someone or if she had any friends at all. I didn't even know if she was still playing her flute."

Rider's sadness washed off him in waves, and Parker felt her heart break for him.

"I can't go back," Rider whispered, sniffling as he wiped his nose on his sleeve. "But I can put an end to Rosamund. I can make sure she never gets her claws into anyone again."

There was a fire in his eyes, and Parker understood now, all that pent-up rage he had in him. She got why he'd left her that note. Why he'd grabbed her and tried to scare her into leaving. It didn't excuse what he'd done, but at least it explained it. He didn't want to see the same thing that had happened to his sister happen to someone else. He wanted to find answers and put a stop to all of it.

"Do you believe me now?"

Parker wasn't sure. She still had to think about it.

Yes, it seemed wild. And Parker had a hard time believing several parts of it. If there was actually a cult in Coronation, would someone have uncovered it a long time ago? Girls couldn't just go missing without a trace. Not anymore. If Parker disappeared, there'd be people looking for her. Someone would notice. No one could cover something like that up.

But then again, maybe they could? Especially if there was something supernatural going on. She'd seen Rosamund in that maze. She was sure of it now. But did that mean . . .

"I don't know," Parker wavered.

"You have to believe me."

Rider's hands shot out and he grabbed Parker by the wrists. He held her tight as he stared into her eyes, trying to convince her.

"You can't let them pull you in," he insisted. "You can't trust them. You have to get out. For your own sake."

"Calm down," Parker said, her voice quivering as she pulled herself from his grip. "I can help you figure out what happened to your sister."

"That's not important right now."

Rider stamped his foot and threw his arms out wide, his frustration spilling over.

"Listen to me," he huffed, his face growing tomato red with the effort. "You need to pack your stuff and go. Tonight. It's not safe for you here."

"Okay," Parker finally mumbled.

But it was only to get Rider off her back. She wasn't going to run away. She had nowhere else to go. She could take care of herself. And she could figure out what had happened to Morgan. At the very least, she needed to try.

CHAPTER
TWENTY-THREE

A picnic on the school's back lawn was a far cry from the initiations and pranks that Parker had been forced to pull at her old school. The food laid out in front of her looked more like a banquet than a school lunch. It was definitely fancier than her sad peanut butter and jelly sandwich that she'd stuffed underneath her knee.

Luckily, none of the girls seemed to notice the crumpled brown-paper bag as they chatted and flounced, leaning over to pick out individual grapes and a handful of almonds, which they promptly popped in their mouths. Parker caught Beth's eye and then dug in herself, grabbing a cracker and a cube of cheese and a piece of salami, which she pressed together and ate in two bites.

"Tennis team bonding!" one of the girls exclaimed, and everyone raised their water bottles and clinked them together.

Parker appreciated the change of pace from her old team. That they could all get to know each other without any anxiety hanging over their heads. There were no conditions she had to meet for her teammates to like her.

"When's our first match?" Parker asked.

"In a few weeks," Beth replied, waving her question off like a fly buzzing around their picnic.

"Isn't that kind of late?"

Parker didn't know the exact timing, but if they didn't have their first games until the end of April, then they wouldn't have time to get more than a few matches in before the school year ended.

"The season's different here," Tory piped up. She was a tall senior who could serve an ace anywhere on the court, a skill that had earned her their number-one singles position.

"But—"

"Don't worry about it," Beth cut in before Parker could raise any more questions. "We'll have plenty of chances to kick some butt out there."

Beth plucked a grape and tossed it across the picnic blanket at Parker. "I can tell you're looking forward to making our opponents cry."

"No," Parker gasped, ducking as she avoided the flying fruit.

"Yes," Beth teased. "I've seen how bloodthirsty you get on the court. You take no prisoners. Which I love."

Parker's face grew hot as the rest of the girls started giggling. But they weren't laughing at her expense. They were laughing with her—impressed by her competitiveness. Appreciative that she put in the effort for the team. And this made Parker smile. It made her feel like she belonged. She reached for another grape but then pulled her hand back sharply as something stabbed into her finger. She yelped, and the rest of the girls turned to her, concern on their faces.

"You okay?" Tory asked.

And Parker quickly nodded. She couldn't let them think that she was a weakling. They'd just been talking about how much of a warrior she was on the court. And warriors didn't get felled by grapes. Unless they were allergic, which she wasn't.

"Just a prick," Parker assured everyone. But once they'd all turned back to their conversations, she flipped her thumb over and examined the damage.

A bright sphere of blood was there on the tip of her finger, and it was only getting bigger. She stuck it in her mouth and sucked, wincing at the salty, metallic taste. It'd felt like a thorn had pierced her. But grapes didn't have those, did they? She looked closely at the bowl of fruit, thinking, and she suddenly remembered that there was something she'd wanted to ask the girls. She didn't know how she could have forgotten about it.

"Did any of you know that kid Rider's sister?" Parker

asked, keeping it as nonchalant as she could, as if she were just wondering about it in passing. "I think her name was Morgan."

Silence fell around the circle as everyone's laughter cut out suddenly. They picked at the food, not eating any of it for a solid minute, until Tory finally spoke up.

"Isn't she the one who died in that accident?"

"Yeah, that's her." Parker nodded solemnly.

"It was so tragic—" Tory began, but Beth cut her off before she could finish.

"Where'd you hear about that?"

"I read it online," Parker lied. She trusted Beth and the rest of the girls, but it was better to be safe. "I can't remember where exactly."

"That's kind of a morbid subject," Beth sniffed, and Parker got the impression that the girl wanted her to drop it.

"Do you all know who she was friends with?" Parker looked around the circle, hoping that someone would have a lead for her. But no one moved. They only shook their heads at her and shrugged their shoulders.

"I think she was a loner," Beth eventually offered. "Just like her brother."

"Yeah, I don't think I ever saw her with anyone," Tory piped up. "She was new to town. It can be hard to make friends."

Was that really all they were going to give her? Parker knew they must have known more. It seemed impossible that no one had ever noticed her. They couldn't have all forgotten about her. Or could they?

"Why the sudden interest?" Beth's question caught Parker off guard and made her lose her train of thought. She turned, not sure what she was going to say.

"Well, I heard that she was the Rose Duchess before me. I guess I was just curious what had happened to her. I read that they never found the body."

"The cliffs can be dangerous," Beth said, her voice flat. "Especially in the dark. And especially if you didn't grow up here."

Parker swallowed, unsure if Beth was threatening her or just being honest.

"Look who's coming over."

Beth's sudden shift to a singsong tone threw Parker off and got the rest of the girls chattering again as they turned to watch Brady making his way toward them, his shoulders wide, his hair tousled, and his tie slightly askew like usual.

"He wants to talk to you." Beth winked at Parker.

"How do you know that?" Parker asked, flustered, feeling put on the spot as the rest of the girls started whispering behind their hands, throwing glances back and forth between the two of them.

"I saw you two sneaking off at youth group."

"We didn't—" Parker blushed. But it was too late to explain as Brady came to a halt right in front of them.

"Can I steal Parker away for a minute?" Brady asked.

And Parker had to give it to him when he didn't hesitate or mumble. He wasn't embarrassed at all. He shot a look around the circle of girls, and when no one opposed, he held out a hand for Parker to take.

"I'll bring her right back. I promise. I just have one thing I need to ask her."

And Parker marveled at how easy it was to take his hand and be plucked out of the group. They strolled off across the lawn while Parker's heart pounded in her chest.

"So what did you want to ask me about?" Parker hoped he couldn't hear how nervous she felt.

"Well . . ." He turned and faced her, pulling her down onto a nearby bench that sat in the shade of a huge dogwood tree.

Above them, its branches spread out, its leaves and white blossoms quivering in the breeze. When Parker squinted, she could just see a light green mist of pollen wafting through the air. Her hand shot up to cover her nose. But as Brady watched her, a curious glint sparking in his eye, she felt suddenly silly. She lowered her hand slowly, coming up with a lame excuse.

"Sorry, I thought I felt a sneeze coming."

"No worries. You okay now?"

When Parker nodded, Brady continued on.

"Have you heard about the bonfire this weekend?"

Flames flashed in Parker's mind, uncontrollable and

hungry. She blinked and could smell the smoke. She could hear the wood cracking in that unbearable heat. She could see herself in the middle of it all, consumed by the fire. Crying out for help.

"Sorry, the what?"

Parker tried to shake the images away. The terrible things she'd seen in her nightmares.

"The bonfire," Brady repeated.

And this time Parker was ready for it as she swallowed down a whimper.

"Is it like a pep rally or something?"

"Kind of." Brady smiled. "It's to celebrate Coronation's birthday. It's the anniversary of when the founders made it through their first year and knew they would survive."

"Sounds fun," Parker mumbled, even though it sounded like exactly the opposite. She had no desire whatsoever to go to a bonfire. She would stay home, and then Beth and Brady could tell her about it after. She was afraid of what she'd do in front of a big fire like that. Probably pass out.

"I was wondering if you wanted to go with me."

The invitation surprised Parker. It stunned her, actually. And she didn't realize her mouth had fallen open until Brady's fingers found her chin and gently closed it.

"You want me to go with you?" Parker asked, not believing a word of it. No one had ever asked her out on a date.

"Unless you're already going with someone." Brady's brow

furrowed, and he looked worried for the first time. Vulnerable. It was an emotion that didn't suit him.

"It's fine if you are. But just—tell me you're not going with Rider."

Rider?

Parker's expression must have given away her confusion, because Brady dove right in with an explanation.

"Beth said that he's been bothering you."

Had she told Beth about Rider? She couldn't remember. And why would she go and tell her brother?

"She was worried about you," Brady said. And he didn't let up. "He's a weird guy. You should be careful around him. That's all I'm trying to say."

"Why don't you like him?" She came right out and asked it. She really hoped it wasn't because he was gay. She liked Brady. How he'd opened up to her at his house. But she didn't mess around with bigots. She didn't tolerate that kind of prejudice.

"He can be—unpredictable."

Parker thought over that last word and wondered why Brady had paused. Did he want to say something else? Did he want to call Rider volatile? Or maybe even dangerous? She'd certainly seen proof that he could be both.

"Do you know about his sister?" Brady asked quietly. "About what happened to her?"

Parker nodded and held her breath, wondering if she was about to get the answers she'd been looking for.

"Well, no one knows where he was that night," Brady explained in a hushed tone. "My dad told me that he saw Rider sneaking back in through the window the next morning when they got there to deliver the news. Some people even wonder if Rider was involved. If, maybe, his parents didn't push for an investigation because they thought it could point back to him."

No. That couldn't be true. Rider wouldn't have lied to her. He wouldn't have done anything to hurt Morgan. Parker had seen how much he cared about her. He could get angry at times, but he'd never go that far.

"I'm not saying he was involved or anything," Brady said. "I just thought you'd want to know."

Quiet stretched between them as Parker thought over everything Brady had said. Was Rider not telling her the truth? Why would he tell her some things and then lie to her about that? She didn't know who to believe. Who to trust. Brady? Rider? Neither of them?

"Thank you," Parker said eventually, still unsure of what she thought about the whole thing. "But you don't have to worry about me."

The quiet opened up between them again, the tweeting of birds and the buzzing of insects rising up to fill the space. The wind rustled the tree branches overhead, and a few dogwood blossoms came loose, wafting down through the clear air. Parker missed it, though, because she was staring at her feet, watching her toes as they wiggled in her sneakers, as she thought about everything that she'd found out over the last couple of days.

"So—" Brady started, and he almost managed to cut cleanly through the awkwardness. "Did you want to go with me? To the bonfire?"

Parker looked up and caught Brady staring at her expectantly. She didn't want to disappoint him. She realized that if someone had told her six months ago that a guy like Brady was going to ask her out, she would never have believed it. This was her chance. And she didn't want to lose it. So she ignored the doubts swirling around in her gut, and she took the plunge, hoping it'd all work out.

"Sure."

CHAPTER
TWENTY-FOUR

"So Brady asked you out on a date?" Parker's mom asked, looking up from her laptop, her blue light–blocking glasses perched at the tip of her nose. She was getting ahead on some work while Parker did her assigned reading at the kitchen table across from her.

"You must be excited. He seems nice."

"It's only a bonfire," Parker said through gritted teeth, already regretting that she'd told her mom about it. "It's not a big deal."

"Well, big deal or not, I think it sounds fun. And I'm glad to see that you're making friends."

She gave Parker a knowing look, which Parker chose to ignore.

"I was worried when we first moved—about how you'd get on without Dani."

Parker's hands clenched around her textbook. She could tell her mom was treading lightly, but she wished she'd stay out of Dani territory altogether.

"But you seem to be doing all right. You're settling in. Making a new home here."

"We all are," Parker replied, and she was happy to see her mom's cheeks color. Happy to move on to a new topic. Only, her mom wasn't done yet.

"You know, Dani's mom called me over the weekend."

Parker tensed again, her jaw tightening, starting to ache. "What'd she want?"

She hoped that she'd sounded innocent. That her voice hadn't trembled with the fear that was shaking through her body.

"She wanted to see how we were doing," Parker's mom said, apparently not noticing Parker's pulse beating away in her neck. "And she mentioned that Dani had gotten into some trouble at school."

Parker's ears rang and the world narrowed to a tiny point in front of her. Her face burned as she remembered that night. As fear and shame rushed into her veins in equal parts.

"She didn't say how, though." Parker's mom held up her hands and shrugged. "But maybe you could reach out to her? See if she's going through anything? Her mom sounded pretty worried on the phone. She said Dani really misses having you around."

"She does?" Parker couldn't mask her shock.

"Of course," Parker's mom laughed. "You two were inseparable. You're best friends. Bonds like that don't break over a move. You'll always be a part of each other's lives, even if you're not as close as you used to be. You know that, right?"

Parker didn't know, but nodded all the same, hoping her mom was right.

"So you'll call her and see how she's doing? It would mean a lot to her mom. And to Dani, too."

"Yeah. I'll give her a call later." If she could muster up the courage to face her. But Parker left that part out. Her mom didn't need to know about their falling-out.

"Sorry I'm so late."

Parker turned as her dad came into the kitchen. His hair was sticking out at a bunch of different angles, but he had a skip in his step. He looked energized.

"There was another emergency at the Rosarium, but I think I might have a lead."

Parker's heart was right back in her throat as she thought about what that could mean.

"We finally caught the guy on camera."

Her dad pumped his fist as her mom gave him a few resounding claps.

"Who was it?" Parker asked, afraid of the answer.

"Well, it's not a clear shot of his face," her dad admitted.

"But I should have enough to ID him once the images have all rendered."

"What will happen when you catch him?"

"He'll probably go to jail," Parker's dad answered absently as he searched through the fridge for something he could eat. "He's done a lot of damage. He even tried to set the office on fire."

"He what?" Parker gasped. Could Rider really be capable of something like that?

"Scary, right?"

Her dad had settled on a slice of pizza and was eating it cold over the sink.

"Luckily, Mrs. York was still in the office that night. She smelled the smoke and was able to put the fire out before it spread. But it could have been really bad. Someone could have died."

And this, Parker realized, was the "unpredictable" Rider that Brady had warned her about. A volatile, dangerous boy who was willing to burn an entire office building down, regardless of whether someone might have been inside. And if he could do that, could he also hurt his sister?

"Don't worry," Parker's dad assured her, mistaking the concern that had clouded her eyes. "We're going to catch this guy before he can do any more damage."

There was a finality in how her dad said it, which made Parker believe him. It was only a matter of time.

Parker just hoped Rider wouldn't do anything stupid.

"I'm going to go make that call," Parker said, grabbing her phone as she got up from the table.

A part of her wanted to tell her dad that the vandal was Rider, but she still didn't know what to think. He was the only one who believed her about Rosamund. If she told on him, she might never find answers.

"Tell Dani I said hi," Parker's mom requested, and Parker assured her that she would as she slipped out the door and headed into the backyard.

When she was by herself, she took a moment to breathe, to try to sort through her thoughts. But it was all a jumble of contradictions and half-truths. She didn't know what, or who, to believe. It was giving her a headache thinking about it.

So instead, she turned to her phone, scrolling through her contacts and clicking on Dani's name. Her finger hovered over the screen, unsure. Then, without giving herself time to back out, she pressed down. She held the phone to her ear and listened as the ringtone sounded. Once. Twice. Three times. The purring echoed in the night before finally cutting out, going to voice mail.

Parker hung up without leaving a message. She wondered if Dani was screening her calls or if she really had just missed it. She could have been in the shower. Or doing homework. Parker raised the phone to try one last time, but a snap drew her attention. Her eyes flickered to the trees that bordered the yard, and she froze, spotting that figure there, its robes rustling in the moonlight, lily white as they flapped.

She lowered her phone and took a step forward, her eyes locked on the woman. Was it the same one who'd been following her? Or someone different? Was she just changing her outfit each night? Parker didn't know, but she kept going, moving carefully, slowly closing the distance.

An inexplicable calm had settled over her. Or maybe she'd just reached her limit. She was too tired to be afraid. Too desperate for answers to worry about what the figure might do to her. She needed to know. And she was ready to risk everything.

She was only fifteen feet away now and the figure hadn't moved. The woman still stood there, her face covered in white makeup, her lips that awful shade of red. She had a hood thrown over her head so that Parker couldn't see her hair. Couldn't tell who she was. But there was something familiar in the way she held her shoulders back. The way she stood tall and proud.

Parker blinked, and suddenly there were two of them. Two figures in white watching her, measuring her approach.

And then there were three.

And four.

They were multiplying faster than Parker could count.

She stopped, her legs quivering underneath her. Her brain shouting at her to get out of there. To run.

She took a step back. And then another. She pushed off, ready to sprint to her house. But she only made it one stride before crashing into the two figures who had materialized behind her.

They grabbed her arms, holding her in tight. And then, before Parker knew what was happening, a hood flew over her head and the world went dark. A hand clamped down on her mouth, muffling her screams. She kicked and struggled to get free. She dug in her heels, but it was no use. She was outnumbered. She couldn't fight all of them off. She couldn't stop them from carrying her away into the night.

CHAPTER
TWENTY-FIVE

Fear had burrowed into Parker's chest, hollowing her out and making a home for itself inside her rib cage. She couldn't breathe or think or speak. Her whole body had locked up. Even if they let her go, she didn't think she could run.

Would her parents miss her? Would they send out a search party? Was this what had happened to Morgan?

The sudden thought sent a new wave of panic coursing through her veins, one last reserve of energy. She bucked against the people holding her, and she managed to connect, elbowing one of them in the side. The person groaned and their grip loosened.

Parker shot forward, not wasting the opening. She broke free of their hold and got a couple of steps in before crashing to the ground, her foot snagging on a root. She rolled over on the ground, her ears ringing, dazed and even more disoriented than before, her hands pawing at the air.

"Here, grab my hand."

And Parker froze, recognizing that voice the second before the hood was whipped off her head.

Beth stared down at her, a concerned look smudging her face. Parker squinted, her thoughts still a mess.

And the other girls—she recognized them, too. They were all wearing the same costumes, but she could see through their makeup now. She recognized Tory and the rest of the tennis team one by one.

"What are you all doing?" Parker croaked.

"It's your initiation," Tory said as she rubbed at her side. "Only, you weren't supposed to put up such a fight. We only got you like a hundred yards before you elbowed me in the ribs."

"Sorry about that," Parker apologized, the tips of her ears turning red. But what had they expected? You couldn't just abduct someone out of their own backyard and expect them not to freak out.

"Beth was a much easier victim."

Tory jerked her thumb at the girl, which caused her to blush.

"So you've been following me this whole time?" Parker stuttered. "Since the Bloom Festival?"

"Only tonight," Tory said.

"But—"

That didn't make sense. They'd been following her for weeks. She'd seen them. They'd been wearing different colors each time, but they were unmistakable with the red lips and the rose crowns.

"Is something wrong?"

"Who are you all supposed to be?" Parker asked, her voice shaking, figuring she knew the answer but needing to hear it all the same.

"We're Rosamund," Tory replied, as if it were obvious.

And it was. But the confirmation only sent chills racing down Parker's back, erasing the moment of relief she'd felt.

"Come on," Tory said, turning so that she was talking to everyone. "I parked around the corner. We can pile in and keep the festivities going at my house."

The girls cheered and followed Tory as she beat a path out of the trees. Their laughter bubbled up around them and echoed through the wooded area, but Parker didn't feel its warmth. It couldn't penetrate the dread filling her thoughts. The doubt and anxiety and exhaustion weighing her down.

"You sure you're okay?" Beth asked, coming up behind Parker. "That was a nasty fall you took. Did you hurt yourself?"

Parker jerked away. But then she softened, seeing the genuine worry written all over her friend's features.

"I'm fine. Just tired, I guess."

"Are you still not sleeping?"

Parker shook her head, wishing she had a different answer.

"Here, take this." Beth rummaged in her pocket and pulled out something that she pushed into Parker's hands. "Carry it with you at all times. It'll help."

"What is it?"

Parker lifted the thing up and examined it in the moonlight, realizing a second later that Beth had given her a small bunch of roses, their stems tied together with a piece of kitchen twine.

"It's posies," Beth explained. "Like in the song."

Parker had to think about that. But eventually it came back to her.

A pocket full of posies.

It'd been one of the lines they'd chanted during the Bloom Festival.

"It's for protection," Beth explained. "They're supposed to ward off evil spirits. And, as an added bonus, they smell really nice."

"They do smell nice."

Parker leaned forward and sniffed the roses, their sweetness filling her nose, cutting through the fog that had settled over her thoughts. And she had to admit that she did feel better. Though that might have been just in her head.

"Remember to keep them with you at all times," Beth repeated.

"Thank you," Parker said as she tucked the posies into her pocket.

And she meant it. It might be an old wives' tale, but at this point, she was willing to try anything.

"So it looks like this is going to be a long night," Beth said, looking ahead at Tory and the rest of the team. "It should be fun, though. Team bonding and all."

"I should text my mom," Parker realized. "Let her know that I went out."

Parker took her phone out, but before she could type a message, an incoming call started lighting up her screen.

"Are you going to answer that?" Beth asked, glancing over Parker's shoulder. And Parker hesitated, not knowing if she was.

"I'll call her back later," she decided, letting the phone go dark in her hand.

"Who was it?"

"Dani," Parker said softly, still staring at the blank screen. "She was my doubles partner—before we moved."

Beth's eyes shifted, and Parker realized that it was the first time she'd seen her friend get jealous. "Do you miss playing with her?"

Parker nodded, a lump forming in the back of her throat. "She was my best friend," Parker admitted as she swallowed her sob down. "I miss everything about her."

"Well, I'll try my best to be a worthy substitute." Beth

threw her arm around Parker's shoulder, and Parker leaned into it, a smile forming on her lips as they hurried to catch up with the rest of the team.

"Thank you," she whispered.

And she felt lighter, the posies working their magic in her pocket.

CHAPTER
TWENTY-SIX

The headmaster's voice droned out from the pulpit, threatening to pull Parker under with its somnolent waves. But for once, she didn't feel the need to fight the drowsiness. She wasn't exhausted or tired or weary. For the first time in a long time, she wasn't afraid.

Because Beth's posies had worked. Parker hadn't expected them to, but when she'd gotten home after the tennis party, she'd tucked them under her pillow, and she'd slept for eight uninterrupted hours. It had to have been the best sleep of her life. She hadn't woken up once in a cold sweat, her sheets and pillowcase drenched and tangled around her limbs. She hadn't gotten out of bed that morning with fresh bruises purpling her arm where she'd flailed in the night and knocked over her nightstand. She hadn't had a single nightmare. She hadn't seen Rosamund at all.

Patting her skirt pocket, Parker squeezed the bundle of roses and relaxed. Even secreted away, the scent filled her nose, giving her a peaceful assurance—a calm that she hadn't felt in weeks. As long as she had her new charm, nothing could go wrong.

"You seem happy this morning."

Brady's breath tickled the side of Parker's neck as he leaned over and whispered into her ear.

"I guess I woke up on the right side of the bed." She curled into him, and he stretched one of his long arms out over her shoulders, looping her into a side hug. Where it had been weird with him under the dogwood tree the other day, it suddenly felt like the right place to be.

He felt so solid next to her. His presence grounded her.

"To round out today's service," the headmaster's voice soared from the front of the chapel, "please join me in communion. If all of you could stand up and form a line."

He swept his arm to the side and everyone started moving. Parker turned to Brady.

"Communion?"

That hadn't been part of any of the chapel services that she'd been to.

"We do it once a month," Brady explained as he got to his feet. "Don't worry. It's just a wafer and some rose water. All you have to do is eat it."

Parker nodded and followed him. She still felt weird about

going through the motions of all these Sower rituals, but she couldn't not participate. Not with everyone watching. Not when she was their Rose Duchess. And it was harmless, wasn't it?

As she waited in line, she spotted Rider a few people behind her, shuffling back in the order, keeping his head down so that no one noticed him. And before she realized it, he'd disappeared altogether, slipping out of the chapel. She wondered what he was up to. Why he needed to sneak away. He was probably furious at her. She'd lied to him. She hadn't run away with her family like he'd wanted her to. But this was her home now. These were her friends. She couldn't turn her back on them. She couldn't leave.

Turning back around, Parker shuffled forward in the line, getting closer to the altar. As she waited, her eyes wandered up to the rose window. She hadn't seen it this close before. But now she could actually make out the scenes depicted in the stained glass. She spotted stories that she recognized from Rosamund's life. The saint's pale figure fertilizing the earth with fish. A ring of girls holding hands and dancing around her. Rosamund springing to life from a beautiful white rose.

But then in the last pane, there was a giant fire. A deadly blaze. And within those flames, someone's arms flailed. Their head tipped back in an excruciating scream, their whole body burning, turning to ash, being devoured by the heat.

Was that Rosamund? Had she died a martyr?

Parker suddenly realized that she didn't know the end of

Rosamund's story. She didn't know how she had died. But before she could think more about it, the line ahead of her moved and it was her turn at the altar.

"Parker."

The headmaster stood there, his hand held out for her to kneel in front of him. When she took her place, he nodded and continued the ceremony.

"We accept this body so that it may grow within us."

He offered her a silver platter and she picked up a wafer, holding the light cracker in her fingertips as she watched him move down the rest of the row. When he reached the end, everyone placed the wafer in their mouths, and Parker followed suit. It dissolved on her tongue, salty and waxy and dry. It sucked all the moisture out of her mouth, making it hard to swallow.

"We drink this so that we may nourish our souls."

The headmaster was in front of her again, this time with a chalice. He tipped it toward her and she took a sip, the rose-infused water flooding her nose with its perfume, the floral flavor pouring into her mouth, washing the wafer's residue away. She swallowed and closed her eyes like she'd seen everyone else do.

Behind her eyelids, though, the world didn't go black. It burst into flames. A scalding heat that she could feel on her face. Flashes of a woman burning. And then a new woman. And someone else after that. She knew they were different by the way they screamed. Piercing shrieks and guttural wails and desperate shouts for mercy.

Parker's fingers dug into the altar. The wood splintered underneath her nails. The smell of smoke overpowered the perfume. Made her want to throw up. Or pass out.

Her eyes finally snapped open and she saw the rose window up above her, the woman engulfed in fire. Just like in her dreams.

Rosamund?

"Rise and go with peace in your heart," the headmaster said. "And know that the cycle continues. That spring will come again."

His words sent a chill through her. Parker looked over at him and swore she saw a sinister bent to his smile. A glint of triumph in his gaze as he stared right back at her. She shivered and stood up, wanting to get out of there as fast as possible. Wondering why the posies hadn't worked.

She looked behind her and saw the bundle of roses lying on the ground. It must have fallen out of her pocket when she'd knelt. She lunged forward and snatched it up, clutching it to her chest.

"You okay?" Brady asked, touching her arm.

"Yeah," Parker replied. "I just think I need some fresh air."

"Do you want me to come with you?"

She did. But she also didn't.

"No. I'll be okay."

She patted him on the shoulder and left him there in the aisle. As she padded out the chapel door, though, she took one last look at the altar. At the headmaster administering his communion to everyone. At the morning light shining down through the rose window high up on the wall.

There was more there, hiding at the core of this idyllic little town. There had to be. But did she really want to dig it up? Did she to really want to know?

She stared at the posies, caressing the red and white flowers, the petals still soft even though they were a day old. Then she pushed through the doors, heading out into the hallway. She made for her locker and spun through the combination. It popped open and she jumped back as an envelope fell out and thudded on the ground. Bending, she picked it up. She had a good idea of who had left it for her, but she didn't know what he would say. She tapped the envelope against her lips, thinking. And then, finally, she decided. She ripped it open and read the note inside.

I have proof. Meet me after school and I'll show you. Don't let anyone see.

Underneath the words, Rider had drawn five of his green beetles marching in a single-file line.

She didn't know if she could trust him. She didn't know if he was telling the truth or if Brady was. But either way, she'd find out that afternoon. It'd all be over soon.

CHAPTER
TWENTY-SEVEN

"You came."

Rider sounded surprised as he opened the door to the classroom and ushered Parker inside. He took a nervous look down the hallway behind her and then closed the door, shutting them in together.

"You could have been clearer on where to meet you."

Parker chose to ignore the alarm bells going off in her head. The last time they'd been in here, Rider had dragged her in against her will. He'd clapped his hand over her mouth and threatened her. Warned her to leave town or else. She didn't like the idea of being trapped in here with him now. She needed to make this quick.

"They're watching us," Rider murmured. "Watching you. They can't know about what I have on them."

"Then show me."

Parker was growing impatient. She was already late for tennis practice. She watched as Rider dug around in his backpack and pulled out a notebook. He flipped it open and she saw the flash of metallic green, his signature beetles crawling across the pages.

"I've been doing research. Looking into the Sowers. And you'd be surprised at how little there is out there on them. This is the only chapter that I could find."

He flipped to the next page of his notebook and kept reading.

"Their principles are based around a saint—"

"I don't need a history lesson," Parker interrupted, pushing his notes aside as she gave him a frank stare. "Do you have proof or not?"

"I do."

Rider fumbled in his backpack again and pulled out a journal. "It's my sister's diary." He held it up for Parker to get a good look. "And her crown."

This last item he handled very carefully. The flowers had dried out and turned brittle over the past year, but it was clear what it had been. The circlet of roses had withered and most of the leaves had fallen off, but the thorns still poked through, their sharp tips more prominent because of the decay.

"It's from when she was named Rose Duchess."

Parker's mouth went dry as she stared at the relic. As she took in the ruined crown of her predecessor.

"What's in her diary?" Parker couldn't keep the curiosity out of her voice.

"See for yourself."

Rider handed her the journal, and she cautiously cracked it open. She skimmed through the first few entries. His sister had only started keeping it when they'd moved to Coronation.

"It seems pretty normal to me," Parker said as she flipped through the pages. Morgan had written about first-day jitters. Worries that she wouldn't make friends. About the girls she'd met in orchestra. About a boy she liked. "Does she write about her friends? Does she say why she went out that night? Who she was going with? Where?"

Rider shook his head. "Well, don't you remember anything?" Parker snapped.

"I told you. I was going through some stuff last year. Figuring things out. I wasn't paying attention to what was going on with Morgan. I wasn't keeping tabs on her."

"But you have to know something."

Parker clapped the diary shut, her frustration spilling over.

"I'm sorry," Rider shouted. "I know I was a terrible brother. That's why I'm trying to make things right."

His outburst startled Parker. It knocked the breath out of her.

So it was guilt that was driving him. Not anger.

She studied him, trying to read his expression.

"Here." Rider turned the pages of the journal and tapped on an entry.

"Everything changed after the Bloom Festival. After she got that crown."

I can't get that song out of my head. "Ring around the Rosie"...Everyone was singing it while we danced. And even though I didn't know the words, I started singing, too. I imagine all of us performing in perfect unison. There was a synchronicity that was so satisfying. We spun and spun and spun and spun, the music going round with us. It felt like I was in a dream, a ballerina dancing in her music box. And no one seemed to mind when I stumbled and fell in the middle of their game. They clapped for me. They gave me a standing ovation and crowned me their Rose Duchess. Now if I could just get that song right. I've tried it on my flute, but it doesn't sound quite the same. Something's missing, but I haven't figured out what.

Parker skipped forward a few days and kept reading.

That song won't leave me alone. It's haunting me. I don't know how much longer I can take it. I hear it in my dreams and during every waking hour. This morning, my pillow was covered in blood. My ears were stained red. But I'm not sure if I inflicted it on myself or if it was something else. Something inside my head. I'm scared. I don't know what's happening to me.

And then.

I see her everywhere I go. I know it sounds impossible, but she's real. Rosie, the woman from the song. She's coming for me. And I'm afraid of what she'll do when she catches me.

The entries got shorter after that. More frantic. And there were some that were completely illegible. But when Parker got to the last one, her fingers went numb. She almost dropped the journal.

I tried fighting her. I tried to escape. But she's in my head. She's in my body. I can't beat her. I can't win. Don't let her take anyone else. Don't let her win. Ashes to ashes... we all fall down.

"See?" Rider pressed as Parker closed the journal.

"But this—it doesn't prove anything."

She didn't want to believe him. She didn't want his sister's story to be true. Because that would make her a target. A victim. That would mean that she was next.

Beginning to panic, Parker fumbled in her pocket. She pulled out the posies and held them to her nose. She took a deep breath and let the scent wash over her. Let it circulate through her lungs. She felt better. Calmer.

"What are you doing with those?" Rider exclaimed.

And before Parker knew it, he'd swatted the bundle of roses out of her hand. It crashed to the floor and exploded on impact, sending petals out in a red-and-white spray.

"Why'd you do that?" Parker shouted as she dropped to her knees and scrambled to gather the rosebuds into her lap. "It was just a charm. A way to keep me safe."

"That's how she controls you," Rider spat out, knocking the petals out of her hands again. "The roses. Their scent. That's how she gets in your head. That's how she brainwashes you."

"But—" Parker sputtered. "I need them. I can't sleep without them."

Too late, Parker realized her slip.

"She's haunting you, too, isn't she?" Rider said, his voice suddenly serious.

"So what?" she snapped, still not wanting to believe him even though a creeping sensation had started to crawl over her. "Bad dreams are bad dreams. Everyone has them. And what about the other girls? What about all the Rose Duchesses who came before? Do you know what happened to them? Do you know where they are now? They can't have all gone missing. Someone would have noticed."

"They have files," Rider sputtered. "At the Rosarium. I've seen them. I can show you."

"How?" Parker challenged him.

"By breaking in."

Parker went silent. She knew Rider's history from her dad. Knew that he'd already broken in several times. Knew that he'd trashed the offices and spray-painted the walls. Knew that he'd tried to set the whole place on fire.

"We can go tonight." Rider puffed out his chest and gave Parker a defiant stare, daring her to back down.

"Fine," Parker exclaimed, getting caught up in the moment and not realizing what she'd agreed to until it was too late. "But this proof better be there. If you're lying to me—"

She let her threat dangle in the air between them, happy to put Rider on the ropes for once. "It's there," Rider assured her. "I promise."

"I guess we'll find out tonight."

And even though Parker hoped that Rider was wrong, deep down she feared that he would be right.

CHAPTER
TWENTY-EIGHT

A chain-link fence rose up in front of Parker, its barbed-wire teeth menacing in the moonlight. Beyond the barrier, she could see the Rosarium, its cluster of greenhouses and offices dark, the workers long departed. For about the hundredth time that night, she wondered what she was doing there. Why had she let Rider rope her into this? She'd been so angry at him earlier that day, and she'd leapt at his challenge. But now she was starting to regret that decision.

What if they got caught? What if Rider didn't find the proof he was looking for and things got out of hand? What if he tried to set fire to the place again? What if his conspiracy theory turned out to be true?

"How many times have you broken in?" Parker asked, trying to get her mind off all the worst-case scenarios running through her head. She was amazed at how calm he seemed.

Didn't he know that trespassing on private property was a crime?

"I don't know." Rider paused and slowly tallied it up on his fingers. "Five or six."

"And they never caught you?"

"Who would break in and mess with their plans? They think they have everyone in Coronation under their control."

Would they really be that confident? It seemed like too big a risk.

"That's why I started leaving my tags," Rider went on. "I wanted them to know someone was coming for them. I wanted them to worry."

Rider crouched down in front of the fence and began rummaging through the bushes. After a minute, he beckoned her over. He had her kneel and motioned for her to crawl through a hole in the chain link as he held it open with both hands.

Staring into that gap, Parker remembered how she'd felt that night when Dani had been caught. When they'd broken into their rival school and cut those tennis racket strings. This was about a thousand times worse. But even though her knees were trembling and her mind was screaming that it was a mistake, she couldn't bail now. She'd already snuck out of the house and trekked across town in the dead of night. And then there were Morgan's diary entries. The nightmares she'd written about. The fact that she had been named Rose Duchess, too. It was all so eerily similar. Parker had to see this through. She had to know.

So she got down on her hands and knees, ducked her head, and crawled through the hole in the fence that Rider must have cut out months ago.

When she got to the other side, she stood up carefully, half expecting a searchlight to snap on. Or an alarm bell to start ringing. Guards to come pouring out of a barracks to apprehend them.

But the night remained calm. And a few seconds later, Rider joined her, brushing his hands on his pants, a grin stretching his lips. Because hadn't that been so easy?

Maybe too easy?

"Here, put this on," Parker insisted, pulling a black handkerchief out of her pocket.

She handed it to Rider and then tied another around her nose and mouth. Her dad had installed cameras. At least this way they wouldn't be recognizable if they got caught on them.

"We should hurry," she said, and Rider nodded, setting off into the complex with Parker right on his tail.

As they crept along the gravel path, Parker couldn't help but wince. The crunch of their footsteps gave them away to anybody who might be nearby. And even though they stuck close to the buildings and minimized their exposure, she couldn't help imagining someone out there watching them, waiting to strike. It was a dark night filled with plenty of shadows, any of which could jump to life and grab them.

An image jumped into Parker's head—a crimson robe flapping—and she spun around, scanning the perimeter. But no one was there. At least, no one that she could see.

"Come on," Rider whispered, pulling her along. "We're almost there."

But as Parker turned back around to keep following, they passed right by the main administrative building.

"Wait, where are we going?" she asked. She'd thought they'd be breaking into the offices, going through filing cabinets and computer databases.

"In there," Rider said, pointing ahead at the smallest of the greenhouses, the one tucked away in the very center of the complex. "That's where they keep all the important stuff. It's where the headmaster has his lab."

Parker remembered the experiment she'd seen behind the man's desk that day he'd called her into his office. But she hadn't thought of him as a mad scientist. She tried to shake the thought out of her head as she stuck close to Rider. The last thing she needed was to imagine the headmaster as a Dr. Frankenstein–like character. She was scared enough already.

As they neared the greenhouses, a chill crept up on her all the same. It ran across her arms and spread over her scalp. It felt like she'd been doused in ice water. It made her numb, slow to react.

All that glass. All those windows. Anyone could be watching them. From anywhere.

The shadows inside the greenhouses shifted. They bubbled and bloomed. Arms and heads and grasping fingers came into shape. They reached for her, scratching against the glass. And Parker couldn't help but remember all those figures in the hedge maze. The scarecrow women with their blank faces and unblinking eyes.

"It's this one," Rider whispered, pulling Parker out of her thoughts. And with some misgivings, she shifted her gaze.

She stood over him as he crouched in front of the door, fumbling with the lock.

"It took me a while to figure out the first time," Rider said as he worked. "But practice makes perfect."

With a flick of the wrist, he twisted the lock and the door clicked.

"After you."

He pocketed the tools he'd used and ushered Parker inside.

"There's not an alarm?" she asked. And she wondered what her dad had been doing since he'd started working there.

"I told you, they think they're untouchable."

Parker didn't like how confident Rider seemed, but she didn't argue with him. Better to go along and get this over with as quickly as possible. So she slipped through the door and waited for him to join her on the other side.

The greenhouse looked even eerier inside. Rows of trellises and flower beds stretched out in front of them, their roses hidden in the dark. But Parker could smell them, the cloying scent stronger than she'd ever experienced, like she'd dunked her head in a vat of perfume. It hung in the air like humidity, thick and oppressive. It made her feel woozy, like she could lie down and take a nap.

She jumped as Rider sneezed, a shot echoing through the vaulted space. She watched while he wiped his nose and swallowed an allergy pill that he'd pulled from his pocket. Then they got to business.

Bending low, they stole through the aisles of roses. Parker kept her eyes peeled, watching for any surprises. She lurched back as a shadow moved out of the corner of her eye. But it was nothing. Just another illusion.

They continued through the greenhouse and only pulled up when they reached a particularly square arrangement of flower beds. Edging around them, they came into a little alcove where it looked like someone had set up a workshop.

Notebooks lay strewn across a table, each filled with diagrams of flowers and charts with crisscrossing lines. Parker squinted and could just make out a list of what sounded like hybrid rose varieties. There were tools as well—miniature shears and tweezers and scalpels and a magnifying glass—and individual pots with seedlings just beginning to sprout.

"This is where he runs his experiments," Rider said

ominously. He raised his arms and Parker thought he meant to sweep everything to the ground, but he got control of himself in time. He let his hands drop back down before he could do any damage.

"Help me look." Rider pointed to the drawers underneath the lab table, and Parker started rifling through them, using her phone's flashlight to see. Her fingers slipped on the card stock and she almost sliced herself open. But she kept at it, glancing through everything.

"What exactly am I looking for?"

"A list of names. Files on families from all over the country. Their targets. Girls like you."

He didn't look up once as he fervently searched.

"They're in here," he mumbled to himself. "You'll see. And then you'll have to believe me."

They fell silent again, each working their way through their own drawers. But Parker wasn't having any luck. All she'd come across were sermon drafts, descriptions of watering schedules, and soil samples.

Beside her, Rider banged one drawer closed and yanked the next open. Parker could feel the frustration radiating off him, but she didn't say anything. She kept her head down and continued to plow through the files. She flipped through receipts and profiles on different rose species. She skimmed a few sheets of experiment notes, each carefully collated with checks for successes and ticks for failures.

"Did you find anything?" Rider asked, his teeth biting off the last of the words.

Parker shook her head. There was a lot there, but nothing unusual. Nothing that resembled the kind of proof Rider had promised her.

"He must—he must have moved it," Rider insisted, his voice ragged at the edges, fraying. "Or shredded it. It was here last time. Names and numbers. All the people they were considering. Everyone I was able to get to and warn crossed off their lists."

"Did you take a photo of the files? Or make copies?" Parker asked. "You must have something."

But as Rider kept up his frantic search, she realized that he didn't. His hands trembled as he fumbled with the drawers, pulling out folders and dropping them back in, pages coming loose and floating to the floor.

"I slowed them down. Sabotaged their plans. I made sure no one accepted their offers. That no one fell for their tricks."

"Rider . . ."

Parker touched his shoulder, trying to calm him down, to keep him from spiraling.

"I'm not making it up," he shouted, shaking her off. "I copied them all down from here. I have the whole list, but I knew you'd have to see it for yourself."

His words echoed through the greenhouse, so loud in the

silence that Parker imagined they could have blown the windows out.

"I swear," he pleaded, his anger burned out, his fight exhausted. "You have to believe me."

Parker held his gaze, noting how gaunt his cheeks looked, how the light had drained from his pupils. Defeat weighed heavily on his shoulders and she barely recognized him.

She reached out a hand to comfort him, to assure him that things would be all right. But right then a blip sounded out in the night and sent Parker's heart pounding against her rib cage.

"We must have tripped a silent alarm," she gasped, spotting the police car as it pulled up outside, its lights flashing red and blue, reflecting through the greenhouse's glass walls.

"We can't run now," Rider grimaced, snapping out of his spiral. "They'll see us."

"What do we do, then?"

This was exactly what Parker had been afraid of. She was going to get in so much trouble. And how bad would it look for her dad? He worked for Mrs. York and now his daughter was breaking into the Rosarium? His daughter was a delinquent?

"We have to wait it out," Rider decided. "They might not find us if we stay hidden."

They didn't really have any other option, so Parker nodded, following Rider as he hunkered down underneath the headmaster's lab table.

Her whole body trembled as they sat there. She was happy

that she wasn't alone, but she couldn't keep the worst-case scenarios from running through her head and accelerating her heartbeat, working her into a panic attack.

"Talk to me," Rider murmured out of nowhere.

"About what?"

"Doesn't matter. It'll distract you. Keep you from worrying so much."

"Well—" Parker grappled to come up with something. "I read online that the Yorks supply roses to the entire East Coast. They're the oldest family-owned nursery in the country."

"About anything but that."

Parker clamped up. She didn't know what to say. But Rider was right. She had to get out of her head. If she didn't get control of her nerves, she was going to freak out and they'd be caught for sure.

"My best friend isn't talking to me."

It was out before Parker had fully thought about it. And she didn't know why she'd gone with that, her most personal secret. It was something that she could barely admit to herself.

"Beth?"

"No. From before. Her name's Dani."

Rider scooted closer, his voice barely a whisper. "What happened with Dani?"

"I left her and now she hates me."

"Your family moved. She can't be mad at you for that."

"I didn't just leave her. I abandoned her."

Parker's voice had dropped so low that she couldn't tell whether she was speaking the words or only thinking them.

"We were meant to be a team," she explained. "We were supposed to have each other's backs. But when we got caught in the middle of some stupid prank, I ran. I got out of there and left her to take the fall. I betrayed her."

"Friends mess up," Rider said. "Brothers, too. Morgan might still be here if I'd been watching out for her. If I'd paid attention." His head dipped and he looked like he was going to say something else. But before he could get it out, a flashlight beam swept over their heads, cutting through the dark and shutting them both up.

Parker's whole body clenched into an even tighter ball as she tried to disappear. She could hear the officers' voices carrying through the greenhouse, growing louder as they got closer. Their lights danced among the flowers as they checked under tables and behind trellises. As they opened a couple of storage lockers and uncovered the fertilizer bins.

Rider's arm wrapped around Parker's shoulder and he squeezed her tight. It made her feel like she wasn't alone. It made her realize that this was what she should have done with Dani. She should have stayed behind, and then they could have faced the consequences together. Like they were about to have to do now.

Only, the officers' voices were suddenly getting farther away. They were searching the other side of the greenhouse.

And then they were moving back toward the door.

One of their radios crackled and Parker perked her ears to listen, just barely hearing the man pronounce it as a false alarm. Her cheeks puffed out as she held in a sigh. And a few moments later, the cops had left the greenhouse. They pulled out of the complex, the gravel spewing underneath their tires.

"Let's go," she muttered, her jaw still clenched. "Before they come back."

"One second," Rider replied as he popped up to his feet, whatever disappointment he'd been feeling before suddenly gone.

"The files aren't here," Parker hissed. But Rider didn't seem to hear her as he reached into his bag and pulled out a can of spray paint.

"Are you really going to do that now? When the police are right outside?"

Parker's eyes bulged as he shook the can, the bead inside rattling as loud as an alarm bell. She could have murdered him.

But instead, she let him finish, one eye trained on the door and the other on what Rider was doing. It only took him a few strokes, and the brilliant green bug had appeared there in the middle of the headmaster's desk, its incandescent wings almost glowing in the dark.

"Happy now?"

But Parker didn't wait for a reply. She grabbed Rider's arm and yanked him out of the lab. They raced through the aisles of roses, Parker keeping her eyes up as she stared through the glass walls, scanning for more cop cars, praying that one hadn't decided to turn back around. They were almost at the door when she caught a flicker out of the corner of her eye. When she spotted that crimson figure watching her. Waiting for her. Rosamund coming to collect.

Parker pitched forward, her foot catching on a trellis. She plummeted through the air, her arms flying out in front of her, searching for anything that could brace her fall. Unfortunately, what she found was the nearest rosebush, and as her palms crashed through the petals and stems, a terrible pain sliced through her body.

She cried out as a thorn stabbed through her flesh, deeper and sharper than she'd ever known. It felt like it was tearing right through her skin and bone to the other side. And in that brilliant white pain, she saw every girl who had come before.

Every single Rose Duchess flashed before her eyes. Mildred Price in her flowing violet dress all the way up to Rider's sister. Their last moments played through her mind in one seamless scene, their screams ringing in her ears, their pain scorching every inch of her body. And then it was Parker's turn on the pyre. Parker's turn to burn. The flames surrounded her. The smoke filled her lungs. This was it. She wasn't going to make it.

"Parker."

Rider's shouts cut through the pain and she realized that he was shaking her shoulders. She tried to focus on what he was saying. She tried to make out the words.

"We have to go," he exclaimed. "They're coming back."

And Parker could hear the siren now. Could see the lights flashing in the distance as the cops raced back toward the greenhouse. She snapped back to her senses and clambered to her feet.

"Come on," she said, and the two of them raced into the night, Parker cradling her hand against her chest, the pain throbbing in her palm as blood dripped down her arm and off the tip of her elbow.

Someone started shouting behind them, but they didn't turn to look. They didn't slow down. They made it to the fence and dove through Rider's hole. They ran as fast as they could down the road, the Rosarium and the cops disappearing in their wake. But the pain, the visions she'd seen, only burned brighter.

CHAPTER
TWENTY-NINE

A yawn escaped Parker's mouth as she stood at her locker the next morning, barely able to keep her eyes open. She swayed forward and then back, wobbling on her feet. Without her posies to keep the nightmares away, she'd slept terribly. This time, though, it hadn't just been the bad dreams keeping her awake. She'd laid in bed all night listening for that knock on her front door, the authorities coming to get her. And she'd had plenty of time to think about everything that had happened.

She still couldn't believe that she'd let Rider convince her to break into the Rosarium. And that they'd come so close to getting caught. She'd risked everything and they'd found absolutely nothing. No names or lists of addresses. No files on the families they'd supposedly lured here before. Not a single shred of evidence.

A part of Parker wanted to believe him. She wanted something tangible that she could blame her bad dreams on. But if his theory was right, there'd be proof. There'd be a paper trail. There'd be other girls and other families. There'd be something more. Other than Morgan's diary, Rider had nothing to go on.

Maybe it really was just bad dreams. Maybe her conscience was punishing her for betraying Dani. Maybe she should have seen a therapist instead of listening to Rider. A doctor could at least prescribe her sleeping pills. Because that was what she really needed. Sleep.

The previous night had been too close a call. She couldn't keep entertaining Rider's conspiracies. She felt bad for him, but she had to do what was best for her. She had to start distancing herself. She had to try to move on.

"Parker."

Her head jerked up at the sound of her name, but she quickly turned away when she spotted Rider rushing down the hallway toward her.

"Parker."

She closed her locker, her hand smarting as she put pressure on it. She'd bandaged it up when she'd gotten home from the Rosarium, but it still hurt. It had throbbed all through the night, her constant companion, a reminder of everything that was wrong.

"Look," Rider said, catching up to her. "I know last night

234

didn't go as planned. But we can still stop them. You can get out before it's too late and I can—"

"Rider," Parker said, her weariness spilling over as she tried to break it to him as gently as she could. "We can't do this anymore. It isn't healthy. For either of us."

"But . . ." Rider faltered.

"I don't want to talk about it," Parker said, squeezing his arm, hoping he understood that she was doing this because she cared about him. She was trying to save him. And herself. "I'm done. Can you please just let it go?"

"No." Rider snatched his arm away from her and plowed right on. "You have to listen to me. Last night was my mistake. The evidence was there before, but they must have moved it."

"Oh, Rider."

"I don't need your sympathy," he snapped, reaching out and grabbing both of her shoulders in a desperate plea. "I need you to listen to me."

"Do you know how much trouble we could have gotten into?" Parker asked, raising one eyebrow.

"I was trying to prove it to you."

"But you don't even know what the truth is," Parker asserted. "We're not in a horror movie, Rider. The Sowers aren't some scary, demon-worshipping cult. It's all in your head. Don't you get that?"

Tears pricked at the corners of Parker's eyes. She felt bad

for laying it all out like that, but someone had to wake him up. Someone had to tell him that he was being delusional. He was hurting himself by chasing after these wild theories. And she didn't want to see him in pain.

She opened her mouth to press on but felt a vibration in her backpack. And then another. The buzzing kept up until it was like a swarm of bees had flown into the hallway. Having no clue who would be trying so badly to get in touch with her, she pulled off her bag and dug through it for her phone.

Beth, maybe? Or her mom? Either way, it was a good distraction, a reason to table this difficult conversation, at least for the moment. But as Parker glanced down at her phone, at the messages piling up one after the other, her breath caught in her chest.

"Is it Dani?" Rider asked hopefully, and Parker had to do a double take. She'd forgotten that she'd told him about her last night when she'd almost had that panic attack. But how could he have guessed she was texting Parker now?

"I messaged her," Rider went on. "I told her that you were in trouble. That you needed her help."

"You what?" Parker's mouth dropped open.

"You wouldn't listen to me," Rider reasoned. "I thought maybe she could convince you. Help you see how much danger you were in."

Parker didn't know what to say. Her mind had gone completely blank. She felt exposed and betrayed. She couldn't look at Rider. So she stared at her phone, watching the messages come in. Then, with a trembling finger, she started reading through them.

> Parker?

> Are you okay?

> Some random guy messaged me saying you needed help.

> He said someone is trying to get you and I was the only one who you'd listen to.

> Is he for real?

> Or is this some kind of prank?

> You left me that night and you've ignored me ever since.

> Now you need me?

> What is happening?

> Say something.

The messages stopped after that, but Parker could see the dots blipping as Dani typed more.

"How'd you even find her?" Parker whispered, her hands trembling.

"You have photos tagged together," Rider said, as if that made it okay.

"You shouldn't have—"

Parker choked up, her fingers curling around her phone, the wound in her palm aching again. She squeezed so tight that her knuckles turned white. She tried to keep it together. She didn't want to seem weak in front of him. She didn't want to show him how much she was hurting.

"I was desperate," Rider blurted out. "It was a last resort. You wouldn't listen to me. I was trying to save you."

Rider's reasons piled up as quickly as Dani's messages had, but they only made Parker madder. They didn't excuse or forgive anything. Rider had pulled Dani into this. Not even her past was safe from him.

"There's no cult!" Parker finally yelled, and students turned up and down the hallway, focusing in on them. "I know you're upset about your sister, but it's all in your head. It doesn't exist. So keep me out of it."

And with that, Parker turned and stormed away, ignoring Rider's shouts as he came after her.

"Parker—"

But that was all he got out. Because suddenly, a pair of

uniformed men rushed toward him from out of nowhere, pushing him up against the wall and pinning his arms behind his back. He struggled against them, but his shoes only slid helplessly along the floor as the men held him in place.

"Is this him?" one of them asked, and the headmaster was suddenly there, too, his hands folded in front of him, a disappointed expression drawing his face down as he looked on.

"That's Rider," he said solemnly. "The one from the video."

"We're going to need you to come with us," the other officer said, and Parker's heartbeat skipped. Because she recognized that voice. She'd heard it the previous night in the greenhouse. And if they were here for Rider, weren't they here for her, too?

She slid over to the wall, pressing her back into the lockers, wishing she could open one and disappear inside.

"Your parents are meeting us at the station."

The officers pulled Rider back and led him down the hallway, his arrest drawing everyone's stares now. Students paused and watched the officers escorting Rider out, whispering to each other, trying to figure out what he'd done.

Parker had other worries on her mind, though. She sucked in a breath as the officers grew closer, and she tried to make herself as small as possible. Her pulse thundered in her ears and she thought they would hear it. That her guilt would give her away. But they didn't even look her way as they walked past. Rider was the only one who noticed her, his eyes locking on hers, one last plea in them. One final warning to get out before it was too late.

CHAPTER
THIRTY

Parker rocked back and forth on the porch swing, her knees pulled up to her chest, hugging herself tightly. Her eyes were glued to the street, her ears perked up to catch the first wails of incoming sirens. Because surely the police would be there soon. She'd avoided arrest at school, but she'd broken into the Rosarium, too. Rider would definitely tell on her. He would cut a deal to save himself. And there was nothing she could do about it. Nothing but wait. They'd come for her soon enough.

She felt oddly numb to it, though. Resigned. She'd escaped something exactly like this once before, so didn't it make sense that she'd get caught now? Wasn't it fitting?

A bleak laugh hiccuped out of her as she imagined what Dani would say. Probably that Parker deserved whatever punishment she had coming. That karma had caught up to her. Or maybe she would understand.

Parker hugged herself tighter as she remembered the responses she'd typed out after they'd hauled Rider away. How she'd been so careful in choosing her words.

> I'm fine.

> It was all a joke.

> Rider has a weird sense of humor.

> Sorry he bothered you.

There was so much more that she'd wanted to say. She'd wanted to apologize for the way she'd left things. For the way she'd let Dani take the fall for their break-in. She'd wanted to ask how the tennis team was doing. To say that she was happy Dani hadn't lost her scholarship. She'd wanted to tell Dani how much she missed her.

But Parker hadn't known how to do any of it. She'd left her apology for so long that she didn't think there was room for forgiveness between them. Not anymore.

Parker startled as a car pulled into their driveway. She scrambled to her feet when she saw her dad getting out of it. He slammed the door and bounded up the path, leaping onto the porch as her mom pushed the front door open and joined them outside.

"We caught him," Parker's dad sang, waving an arm in the air as he roped Parker's mom in and kissed her on the cheek. "Got him on tape and everything."

Parker's stomach sank as she realized what he was talking about.

They had video of Rider breaking in. Which meant they had video of her, too. So Rider didn't need to tell on her. They already had her red-handed.

"That's exciting," Parker's mom exclaimed, patting her husband on the chest. "Who was it?"

"Just some local kid."

Parker did her best to avoid eye contact with her dad, picking at her bandaged hand instead. She'd told her parents that she'd broken a glass. That she'd accidentally cut herself on the shards when she went to pick it up. But her dad would know the truth. He'd have it on tape.

"You should have heard the story he'd come up with, though," her dad went on. "It was wild. He'd concocted this whole conspiracy theory that the Yorks were leaders of a cult that performed human sacrifices."

"Where'd he get that?" her mom asked.

Parker's dad shrugged. "Probably from the internet. I spoke with his parents and they said he's been having a hard time coping since his sister died last year in an accident, and it sounds like he took it pretty hard. I guess he's still grieving. Trying to make sense of it all."

The three of them fell quiet. Hearing Rider's parents' side of things made Parker feel a little better. But it also made her feel worse. It made her wonder if she could have helped him more. If she should have told someone. Then maybe he would have gotten the help he needed before everything had spiraled out of control.

"Is dinner ready?" Parker's dad asked, changing the subject to something happier.

"Almost."

Parker's mom wiped her hands on her apron and Parker realized that she had flour dusting her hair and smeared across her nose. It was strange to notice how her mom had transformed, cooking meals from scratch when they'd lived off takeout and canned soup a lot of nights back in the city.

"I just have to put the biscuits in the oven."

"You go ahead," Parker's dad said, ushering her toward the front door. "We'll meet you inside."

Parker's mom didn't seem to notice anything strange in the request, but as she swooped back into the house, Parker's dad turned to her, the celebration of before gone from his face.

"Is there something you want to tell me?"

His brow furrowed as he crossed his arms over his chest and gave her a stern look.

"I—" Parker stuttered, losing steam before she'd gotten herself started.

Of course he knew. He oversaw the security system. He'd

installed the cameras and probably reviewed all the videos, too. He had to have seen her breaking in. He had to know she was a part of this.

"Stop." Her dad raised a hand. "I deleted the footage, and Rider didn't say anything about having an accomplice. So no one knows you were there, and I'd like to keep it that way."

Parker's shoulders slumped. Her head dipped as relief washed over her.

"But I'm disappointed in you," he said. "I thought you were doing well with the move. I thought you were getting a fresh start here like your mother and me. Has it been hard? Are you missing your old school? Your old friends? Do you want to go back?"

"No," Parker sputtered, her head snapping up. "Everything's great here."

And it felt like a betrayal to say it. Like she'd completely turned her back on Dani with that admission.

But it was true. She didn't want to go back. She'd decided that last night. Coronation had everything she needed. It had friends and a new school. It had homespun festivals and nature everywhere. Most importantly, it was a place where she fit in. Where she felt like she belonged. Despite all the bad dreams and hallucinations, she didn't want to give that up.

"That was just a blip," Parker promised. "A mistake. It won't happen again."

"Why did you tag along with him?"

Her dad had asked the one question she didn't want to answer. The one that she couldn't, not without sounding just as delusional as Rider.

"It was a dare."

Parker twisted her fingers, hoping her dad couldn't see through the lie.

"Well, it's okay now," he finally said. "Just don't do it again."

And with that, he patted Parker on the shoulder and gave her a kind smile.

"I know peer pressure can be tough. But be smarter in the future. This is your one free pass. You'll be in serious trouble next time something like this happens."

"Thank you," Parker squeaked. And then she reached up and gave him a hug. "I won't let you down again."

And she meant it. She knew that her dad had risked his job to delete that footage. And she appreciated it more than he could know.

"I think you have a visitor," Parker's dad said, suddenly distracted by something behind her.

And as they pulled out of their hug, Parker turned and saw Brady standing there at the edge of the porch.

"I didn't mean to interrupt—" He broke off.

"Can I?" Parker asked, holding her question out until her dad nodded.

"Dinner soon," he said as he turned to go into the house. "Brady's welcome to stay if he likes."

Parker waited for the front door to shut, and then she padded down the porch steps, meeting Brady on the lawn.

"What's up?" she asked, feeling suddenly lighter than she had in weeks.

"I brought you something," Brady said, his hands held behind his back. "But you have to guess."

"I don't know." Parker mulled it over for a few seconds. "Cupcakes?"

"Close," he chuckled. And then with a ta-da, he pulled out a small bunch of roses.

"Are those posies?" Parker exclaimed, surprised that Brady would have thought of it. "Beth gave me one of those."

"I kind of got the idea from her." Brady blushed. "Do you like it?"

"It's perfect," she said, and she skipped forward to take it from him, breathing in its aroma, feeling a peacefulness wash over her almost immediately. "I'll make sure to keep it safe."

And she tucked it into her pocket, just like Beth had taught her.

"So," Brady started, drawing it out like he expected her to understand what he wanted to say from that one syllable alone.

"What?"

"Are we still on for the bonfire tonight?"

"It's tonight?" Parker chirped. She couldn't believe she'd forgotten about it.

"Yeah."

Parker was shocked that he sounded so nervous. So uncertain that she'd say yes. Which made her realize that he cared. He really wanted to go with her.

"I can't wait," she exhaled. And then she got another lungful of the roses as she sucked in a deep breath.

At first, the idea of the bonfire had scared her. She didn't want to be around all those flames. Not after the nightmares she'd had. And she didn't know what to expect from Brady. She'd never been on an actual date. She'd worried that she'd mess things up.

But she was tired of looking over her shoulder. Tired of expecting the worst. She was ready to let it all go. She was ready to have some fun. And she'd start tonight. With Brady.

"I'll pick you up in an hour?" he asked, and Parker nodded, watching him go, the posy back under her nose, enveloping her in its scent even though she didn't remember pulling it back out.

CHAPTER
THIRTY-ONE

The sun was on its way down when Brady and Parker sauntered through the garden entrance, making their way along the now-familiar paths. They followed the music, the clink of glasses, the clamor of people joking and talking and having a good time until they came out into the same clearing where they'd held the Bloom festivities just a few weeks ago.

"Her Highness returns," Brady declared, the gesture tickling Parker as he unfurled his hand dramatically, a courtier announcing her arrival.

And as his words carried out over the crowd, the din suddenly died down, everyone turning to look her way, their eyes scanning her up and down. She blushed and fiddled with her skirt. She'd borrowed the flowery sundress from her mom, and she hoped it looked good. She hoped it was appropriate.

"Don't worry about them," Brady leaned in and whispered.

He put his arm around her waist and drew her in close. "You're their Rose Duchess. They worship you."

And for a fleeting second, Parker believed that maybe they did.

But then reality came crashing back in. All those eyeballs became too much. Her cheeks burned red hot, and she had to start fanning herself to get some fresh air. She wasn't used to the spotlight.

"You made it," a voice sang out, and suddenly Beth was right there beside them. "And I see you're in good company."

She nodded at Brady and spun around, a ball of energy, her usual bubbly self somehow more electric tonight, a fire-cracker waiting to go off.

"I'm going to steal her away for just a minute," Beth said.

She took Parker's hand, gently tugging her out of Brady's hold. She hugged her and Parker could suddenly breathe again. She looked around and noticed that everyone had turned back to their conversations. Which made her wonder if she had only imagined their earlier stares.

"Come on. I want to show you something."

Beth set off, pulling Parker into the clearing. Parker focused on Beth's hand, recalling the "Ring around the Rosie" game. She didn't let go as they weaved through the tables of food and skipped around fellow revelers. She held on tight as the celebra-tory mood seeped into her bones, as the wind played with her hair and twirled her skirt. As the garden scents swirled all around her. She saw that Beth was walking barefoot and suddenly had the urge to do the same. So she kicked off her shoes and didn't even look to see where they'd fallen in the grass. With the dirt beneath her feet she felt connected to the community, to the history of this place. And when Beth started dancing, she couldn't help but join in.

When they made it to the center of the clearing, Beth pulled up short and their dancing slowed. The statue of Rosamund wasn't there this evening, but it had been replaced by a large pile of wood. The jagged shards rose up from the ground like teeth, piercing the sky, and Parker could smell the gasoline waiting to be ignited.

"They'll light it as soon as the sun goes down," Beth said as she looked up to the sky, gauging how long that would take. "It's almost time. But first—" Beth whipped around, barely able to contain her smile. "Your surprise."

She took Parker's hand again and led her around the unlit bonfire to where a statue stood all by itself, just like the one they'd danced around at the Bloom Festival. Only, it wasn't Rosamund.

"Is that—supposed to be me?"

Parker came up short, letting her hand drop from Beth's grasp as she stared at the thing in front of her.

It wore what looked like a tennis skirt, the white material made from lilies, the halter top exposing two athletic arms, the branches that had been used doing an eerily good job of mimicking muscle. The tendrils of brown-thatch hair sprouting from its head had been pulled back into a tight ponytail, and the whole figure stood crouched in a split stance, as if preparing to return a serve.

"Of course," Beth chirruped, delighted, as if she'd put the thing together herself. "You're our Rose Duchess. You should feel honored."

"What are they going to do with it?"

Parker had edged closer. She couldn't help herself. It was uncanny how much it resembled her.

"Don't you remember the story?"

Parker thought she did. But she didn't know the end. She didn't know exactly what had happened to Rosamund. So she shook her head, a little afraid of what the answer would be.

"She sacrificed herself," Beth said, her earlier cheer suddenly gone. "She gave up her life in order to provide for everyone else."

A chill crept up Parker's neck as Beth's eyes flitted over her shoulder to the cold bonfire behind them. The stained-glass image flashed in her mind, the one she hadn't recognized from the headmaster's stories, the woman in the middle of the flames, her arms flailing for help.

"And just like Rosamund," Beth went on ominously, "each year the Rose Duchess follows in her footsteps. Takes her place. Offers herself up for the good of the whole."

Parker's eyes bugged out and her breath caught in her

throat. She did a double take, her head snapping from the stacks of firewood to Beth to the statue they'd created of her. Rider couldn't have been right. They weren't about to burn her alive, were they?

"It's only symbolic." Beth broke finally and she let out a laugh. "Your statue gets set on fire, not you."

Parker nodded slightly as she rubbed the back of her neck. Her body was still shaking, and she hoped Beth couldn't tell. The story had been so close to Rider's. It made sense now how he'd come up with it.

"I'm going to go find Brady," she eventually mumbled, wanting to get as far away from her statue as she could.

"I'll see you later," Beth said, letting her go. "I want to get a better look at this thing. I mean, it's you. How cool is that?"

As Beth took a step closer to the statue, Parker backed away. She didn't like the idea of watching herself go up in flames, even if it was tradition. It was a little too much like the nightmares she'd been having.

Edging away, Parker put some distance between herself and her floral twin. When she reached the other side of the bonfire, she started glancing around for Brady but didn't see him anywhere. Not at the punch bowl or near the platters of appetizers. Not on the dance floor or standing with his friends from the lacrosse team. She kept scanning, and then she suddenly came up short. Her pulse beat one loud note against her eardrum. Her hand fluttered to her mouth as a gasp came out.

But it couldn't be. She couldn't have—

Parker scrambled forward, pushing people aside, craning her neck to see through and over them all. Were her eyes playing tricks on her? Was it another hallucination? It had to be, didn't it? Because it was impossible. Dani couldn't be there. She couldn't have traveled all the way up to Coronation. She wouldn't have. But there she was, scanning the crowd, looking for—

"There she is, the guest of honor."

The headmaster opened his arms wide and pulled Parker over, derailing her from her search as he greeted her. Mrs. York and Brady were there with him, too, and Parker didn't know how she'd missed him before. But she didn't have time to talk. She had to find Dani. She had to make sure she hadn't imagined it.

"I'm so glad that you could make it tonight," the headmaster continued. "We wouldn't be able to celebrate properly without you here."

He paused then and looked up. Parker followed his gaze and saw that the sun had sunk to the horizon, only the last aura of orange still visible in the evening sky.

"I do believe that it's almost time to begin," he said. And with that, he let Parker go, striding off toward the bonfire.

"Good luck tonight," Mrs. York said. The woman squeezed Parker's hand and followed her husband, leaving Parker to wonder what exactly she needed luck with.

"Are you okay?" Brady asked, holding his hand to her fore-head as if she might have a fever.

"I saw Dani," she blurted out. "Or, at least, I think I did. She was in the crowd, but I can't find her now."

"Dani?"

And Parker remembered that she hadn't told Brady about her. She hadn't told anyone except for Rider and Beth.

"She's from DC," she explained quickly. "She was my best friend—before we moved."

"I'll help you look for her," Brady said. Parker was relieved that he understood. That she didn't have to explain it all to him. "After the ceremony."

She glanced up then, looking to the bonfire, feeling an uneasiness blossoming inside her. Everything about this night felt off. The crowd and the statue and the headmaster standing up there about to address them all.

"Are they really about to burn me at the stake?" she leaned in and asked, her voice a whisper. "Burn my statue, I mean."

"It's tradition," Brady said, mimicking her hushed tone. "They've been doing it for centuries."

Parker was about to ask him more, but she got cut off as the headmaster's voice boomed out over the clearing, everyone growing quiet as they turned to listen.

"Welcome. Welcome. It's so good to see you all. My friends. My family. My fellow Sowers. And, of course, our Rose Duchess."

His hand stretched out toward Parker and she felt

everyone's eyeballs searching for her again. Instinctively, she shrank back, doing her best to disappear behind Brady's broad shoulders.

"As we celebrate our community's anniversary, I'm reminded of Coronation's first days. I'm reminded of stepping foot on a desolate beach in an unknown world. Of having nothing. Of wanting everything."

Parker marveled at how well he spoke. At how he controlled his audience and how he drew them in. It was almost like he was sharing his memories. Like he'd been there among the first settlers all those years ago.

"It took a lot to get our settlement off the ground. It took blood and sweat and hard work. It took tears and time. It took pain and punishment and grief. It took sacrifice to build a new home."

There that word was again. Sacrifice. The theme of the night. The theme of the Sowers. And as it left the headmaster's mouth, two men came around the bonfire and planted Parker's statue right in the ground.

"Rosamund saved us all those years ago. She taught us how to work the earth. How to make it through the winter. And when that wasn't enough, she made the ultimate sacrifice. She died so that we could go on. Her ashes sowed our fields. They ensured our survival. And so we honor her tonight as we honor her every year. We give thanks and ask for another year of blessings."

The crowd erupted in applause, the sudden crackling like fireworks going off overhead.

"Parker?"

Her name echoed through the clearing, and she whipped around to see the headmaster holding his hand out for her, beckoning her to hear his call.

"Will you join us?"

The crowd parted, and an aisle opened up, running straight to the headmaster. To his outstretched hand. To the bonfire beyond. And in that moment, Parker's world started to spin. Her vision blurred and she felt suddenly light-headed. Her cheeks went dead cold as all the blood drained out of them.

"I'm—I'm not feeling well," Parker mumbled, speaking to Brady as she turned away from the bonfire. "Can you take me home? I need to lie down."

"It's fine," Brady whispered back to her. "You're fine. Come on. There's nothing to be worried about."

He took her hand and started forward, pulling her in the opposite direction from where she wanted to go.

"I can't," Parker shouted, though it came out as a whimper. She ripped her arm out of Brady's grip and tried to run away.

But she could only stumble. She could only make it a few steps before she had to bend over at the waist and take a break. She couldn't breathe. She couldn't think. Her legs wavered underneath her and she dropped to one knee.

"It's going to be okay," Brady whispered. But Parker wasn't sure that she believed him.

That familiar sickly-sweet aroma wafted under her nose, and she saw that he'd taken the posies out of her pocket. She watched as he toyed with it, a smirk marring his lips, distorting his features into something ugly. Into something evil. And she wanted to cry. Because she realized, finally, that Rider had been right. She should have listened to him. She should have left. She should have gotten out when she had the chance.

"Help—" she muttered, her mouth dry, her tongue cracking.

But her words fell away as her head swooned. As her eyes dipped closed. As her body tilted forward. As the world went dark around her and she crashed into the ground.

CHAPTER
THIRTY-TWO

The smell of gasoline clawed its way up Parker's nose, the acrid scent choking her, blocking her airway. She gasped and her eyes fluttered open. But everything around her was dark and fuzzy. She didn't know where she was. She couldn't remember where she'd been. Her head ached and her mouth had gone bone dry. She tried to shout, but no sound came out. She tried to move, but something held her fast.

Parker's head spilled to one side and she squinted through the daze. She was just able to make out a length of rope trailing over her shoulder and across her chest. Wrapping around her whole body, tying her down.

And then she heard the snap of a twig. She saw the figure materialize in front of her, its white robe flapping in the night air. Its hand was held high, bearing a torch that flickered and cast shadows across its face. Shadows that did nothing to hide the horror that Parker knew so well from her nightmares.

She lurched back, desperate to get away. She jerked against the ropes, her heart beating wildly in her chest, fear sizzling through her veins. But her bonds held fast. She couldn't move. Not even an inch.

"Wake up. Wake up. Wake up."

She whispered it to herself, her eyes shut as she tried to will the nightmare away. This was just another dream. Like all the rest. This wasn't happening. It couldn't be—

"And with another year passed, we give thanks to you, Rosamund, our savior and protector."

Parker lifted her head as the headmaster's voice cut through the haze. She started to rouse from her stupor and the night became clearer around her. Details stood out. Faces swam into focus. And the figure that she'd thought was Rosamund turned into the headmaster.

"We offer up our Rose Duchess and ask for your continued blessings. We honor you with her sacrifice."

Parker's eyes grew wide as the headmaster's torch flickered in the night, the flame dancing in his eyes, illuminating the crowd beyond him.

"Ashes, ashes."

The chant rumbled in the background.

"Ashes, ashes."

Parker saw them all, their hands linked, their mouths

moving, the crowd speaking as one. She spotted Beth and Brady. Then Tory and the rest of the tennis team. Their faces moved in the crowd. She watched them spinning. Chanting with everyone else. What were they doing? Hadn't they been her friends? But as hard as she looked, she couldn't find Dani.

"Ashes, ashes."

She couldn't tell if they were spinning around her or if her mind was spiraling out of control. She strained against the ropes holding her tight. She tried to kick out with her legs. She opened her mouth and screamed, but no one seemed to care. No one seemed to hear her.

This couldn't be happening. This couldn't be reality. It was all a dream. A nightmare. She continued to struggle, but it was no use. She wasn't waking up. She wasn't getting out of here. She was about to burn.

"We all fall down."

As the crowd finished the chant, the headmaster came forward and held the torch high over his head. Then, with a careful, ceremonial dip, he dropped the flame into the stack of kindling. He watched as the gasoline lit, as the bonfire started to burn.

"You can't do this," Parker gasped, the heat of the flames catching on her cheeks. "You can't—"

The words stuck in her throat as she inhaled a lungful of smoke. She coughed and spat. She kept fighting to get free.

Because the headmaster wasn't listening to her. No one was. Something sliced into her palm, and she turned it over to see blood seeping through her bandage. It covered her hand, bleeding faster than it should.

Then, just like the night at the Rosarium, she heard their screams. They welled up around her. They swallowed her whole. Their faces flashed through her mind as the pain of every Rose Duchess who had come before poured into her, scraping her raw until she couldn't bear it.

Parker stomped her feet and dug at the ropes with her fingernails. She strained against her bonds, but she couldn't move them. The flames were licking at her toes, consuming the wood faster than she thought possible. She didn't have much time left.

With a last, frantic burst of adrenaline, she shoved her whole body against the stake she was tied to. She threw herself into it, pushing with her legs, praying that something would give.

But nothing did. And she was only wearing herself out faster.

And in that moment, she heard it: Dani's cries.

"Stop! Please, stop! Parker!"

Sweat streamed down Parker's forehead and tears leaked from her eyes. The smoke billowed up around her, blocking her view of the crowd. She inhaled and it rushed into her lungs. She gagged and almost threw up.

"Let me go!" Dani's voice echoed through the chants. "Let me—"

Parker thought she might suffocate before she burned, and she didn't know which would be worse. The flames were closing in on her, forming a circle that surrounded her, spinning round and round.

Ashes, ashes.

She'd be with them soon. With Morgan and all the Rose Duchesses who'd come before. And there would be more to come after. A continuous cycle. She couldn't stop it. It was out of her control. She could only let the flames take her, like they had so many times in her nightmares.

Exhausted, Parker tilted her head back and opened her mouth wide. She screamed with everything she had left, howling into the night. Would her parents hear her? Would they wonder what had happened when she didn't come home? Or would the headmaster get to them, too? Explain it all away with a story about some terrible accident.

It didn't really matter. She wouldn't be around to see it. She—

A *crack* shot off in the night. And then another. Parker dropped her head back down as she heard the crowd's chanting waver, their words turning to mumbles and shouts.

The wind picked up, the smoke cleared, and Parker could see the headmaster in front of her, his solemn expression gone.

Another *crack* popped, and he turned away from her,

shouting out orders, clearly flustered. Something was happening. Something he hadn't planned on.

Parker leaned forward against her ropes and strained to see through the night.

The crowd was dispersing, clearly confused and maybe a little afraid. Another *crack* went off and someone screamed.

"Hold on. I'm going to get you out of here."

Parker hadn't seen him come up behind her, but she knew Rider's voice. Somehow, he'd gotten away and come to rescue her. She couldn't believe it. It wasn't over yet for her. She heard him kicking logs to the side, and then he was next to her, crouched low, his fingers tugging at the rope.

"Hurry," she urged, her eyes scanning the crowd. "Before they see you."

"I've got that covered."

And Parker saw him reach into his pocket and pull something small out. He held it to the flames and then hurled it out into the crowd. An explosion rocketed through the air a few seconds later, causing more people to panic and scatter.

"Firecrackers," Rider explained, and Parker remembered how he'd been playing with them that day on Main Street.

"I've almost got it."

Parker gasped as the rope's tension eased and her hands came free. She scrambled to unwrap herself from the stake, and then she was following Rider, moving along the small path he'd cleared in the bonfire to get to her.

"A parting gift."

Rider pulled up short and tossed two handfuls of fire-crackers into the blaze. Then they turned and booked it out of there, getting a few yards away before the miniature bombs went off, exploding in rapid succession, popping like gunfire.

They ducked low and made for the edge of the clearing, using the mayhem as cover.

"You came for me?" Parker stumbled over the words, but at least she was tripping over them and not her feet.

"I wasn't going to let them get you like they got my sister."

"But how did you get away? They caught you. I was there."

"They couldn't keep me in a cell. I'm a minor. And I've been sneaking out of my house for months to break into the Rosarium. So stationing a couple of cops out front wasn't exactly going to stop me."

Parker didn't know what to say. She didn't know how to thank him. He'd risked his life to save her. He'd climbed through that fire and cut her loose. There was a mob of people looking for them now, willing to do anything to get to her, to end anyone who stood in their way.

"Where do you think you're going?"

Parker froze as Beth's shout carried over the commotion in the night. She was standing right there in their path at the edge of the clearing, the smile plastered on her face more unhinged than beatific. Parker grabbed Rider's hand and started to drag him in the opposite direction. They couldn't afford to stop now. If they drew attention to themselves, they'd never get out of there. As it was, the confusion that Rider had caused with his firecrackers was starting to wear off. The smoke that had filled the air from the mini explosions was dissipating. Pretty soon the crowd wouldn't be distracted. Pretty soon there'd be nowhere to hide.

"Not so fast." Brady stood on their other side, his arms laced across his broad chest, an impenetrable wall. Because while Parker had a chance against Beth, Rider had no shot to take down Brady.

"I trusted you," Parker whimpered. "We were partners. I thought you were my best friend."

"We can still be best friends," Beth said simply. And Parker realized that the girl meant it.

"But you're with them. You want me dead."

"Being the Rose Duchess is an honor. Your sacrifice ensures our future. Your memory will live on with us forever."

"Parker, run!" Rider yelled. And before she knew what was happening, he rushed Brady, shouting a battle cry as he lunged for the bigger boy.

For a moment Rider was on top of him, keeping him down with an array of blows. But it only took one miss for Brady to recover from the surprise attack. He threw Rider off easily, tossing him to the side like a toy. And when Rider made to get up, Brady was on top of him. His foot sank two inches into Rider's stomach, causing the boy to let out a strangled scream as he spat up a mouthful of blood and bile.

"Get off him!" Parker streaked forward, her nails flying out in front of her, scraping across Brady's cheek. Blood streaked from the scratches, but it was only a flesh wound. It wouldn't stop him. It wouldn't even slow him down.

Something whirled past Parker's head and she jumped out of the way just in time. The metal clanged against the ground and Parker saw that Beth had picked up a garden shovel. She pulled it back and swung again, but this time Parker was ready for it. She caught the shovel's wooden shaft in midair and kicked out with her leg, hitting Beth right in the stomach, dropping her to the ground with one blow.

Not wasting a second, she turned and swung the shovel like a tennis racket, her excellent hand-eye coordination making sure that she connected with her target. The metal boomed like a gong as Brady's head snapped back and he crumpled to the ground.

Parker dropped the shovel and knelt next to Rider, tapping him on the shoulder.

"Are you okay?"

Rider wheezed and wiped the spittle from his mouth.

"Yeah," he coughed as he sat up. "Let's get out of here."

But as Parker helped him to his feet, she heard a familiar voice shouting somewhere in the night. She turned and saw Dani, unmistakable in the moonlight, her dark ponytail bobbing up

266

and down, her head shaking like a bobblehead as she grappled with Sister Florence.

"Leave her alone," Parker yelled.

And in that moment, the two girls' eyes met and the weight of Dani's showing up there hit Parker almost as hard as the shovel had when it collided with Brady's head. Her knees buckled and she almost went down. Because even after everything, Dani still cared. She'd come all the way to Coronation for her.

"We have to go," Rider urged Parker, but she ignored him, brushing him off. He must not have seen. Parker couldn't leave now. She couldn't leave without Dani. Her best friend needed her. And she wouldn't disappoint her again.

"I have to help Dani," Parker shouted, pointing toward the girl. And before Rider could stop her, she took off, racing to her best friend, reaching to bridge the distance that had sprung up between them.

But before she'd gotten halfway there, a strangled cry escaped Dani's mouth. Her head jerked up as Sister Florence yanked her by the ponytail, as she pressed the tip of her long garden shears into the girl's back and entered the maze.

"No—"

Parker sprinted to catch up, but she was already gone.

"What are you doing?" Rider screamed, yanking her back. "You can't go in there. It's too dangerous."

"I have to," Parker sobbed. "I won't abandon her. Not this time."

"Wait—" Rider yelped.

But Parker didn't let him finish. She pressed forward without him, moving across the gardens and through the entrance, those terrible green walls rising up around her. She didn't give herself time to think about what was waiting in there for her. She didn't let the fear overcome her. As she wound down the paths and through the maze, losing herself in the twists and turns, she focused on finding Dani. On rescuing her best friend.

CHAPTER
THIRTY-THREE

It didn't take long for the maze to swallow her.

As Parker rushed through the narrow corridors, turning left and right and left again, she hunted for signs of Dani. She called the girl's name, listening for the sounds of a scuffle, for a scream or labored breathing. For anything that would point her in the right direction. They couldn't have gone far. The old woman had to drag Dani in. And Parker knew that her best friend would put up a fight. She'd scratch and claw with everything she had. Parker would find her. She had to.

But what if she made a wrong turn?

Parker came up short, her panting filling the night. She stood in the middle of a crossroads, four paths shooting out around her, disappearing into darkness. She didn't know which to choose. She didn't know which was right. If she got turned around, if she got lost, she could be wandering around in here for days. She might never find Dani.

Parker closed her eyes and set off, heading straight. Indecision wasn't going to help. She had to choose and keep moving. She couldn't stop, no matter what.

"Not that way."

Parker felt a hand pulling her back, and she turned to see Rider standing behind her, his phone's flashlight lighting up the night, trained on the map he'd pulled out of his pocket. The one he'd created on his own. It looked like he'd filled in more since the last time Parker had seen it, but the middle of the maze was still blank.

"I assume she's heading to the center," Rider said, tapping the paper. "Which means we need to take this one."

"Thank you," Parker whispered. "You didn't have to—"

But Rider had already set off, blazing a trail through the hedges, checking his map every few seconds as he navigated them deeper into the abyss.

They took a left and then a right and then a left again. And even though Parker had been in here once before, nothing looked familiar. If Rider hadn't come after her, she would have gotten turned around for sure. She was dizzy even now, her head spinning as they twisted and wound their way along the paths, taking a route that she knew she couldn't replicate. That she couldn't find even with a bird's-eye view.

"Are we getting close?" Parker asked after several minutes of taut silence.

Her feet hurt and she was out of breath. She needed to take a break. But she knew that if she stopped, the whole night would come crashing down on her. The bonfire and the chanting. All those people she'd thought were her friends turning on her.

"We're almost at the end of what I have mapped out," Rider said, pulling up short, slowing their pace.

"And after that?" Parker asked, worry squeezing her stomach until she thought she might throw up.

"After that, we guess."

Parker faltered, her knees shaking. A helpless moan escaped her lips. They couldn't leave it up to chance. They couldn't—

Parker gasped and backed away.

"What are you doing?" Rider asked, confusion knitting his eyebrows.

"Don't you see it?"

Parker's finger trembled as she pointed down the row, singling out the figure standing there in the shadows, waiting for them, the hem of its dress fluttering in the breeze.

"What is that?" Rider asked, and a part of Parker was relieved that he could see it, too.

"It's her," Parker whispered. "We have to go. We have to—"

But something strange happened then. Just as Parker was

ready to sprint away, the figure raised its head ever so slightly and gave her a gentle nod, beckoning her to follow as it disappeared around the corner. And before Parker could convince herself not to, she plunged after it, pulling Rider along behind her.

They played this follow-the-leader game for another few minutes, slipping through the maze, neither party making a noise. But every time Parker and Rider turned the corner into a new corridor, the figure was there, waiting patiently for them, standing out of reach until, just as suddenly as the figure had materialized, it was gone.

"Where'd it go?" Rider asked, looking up and down the path but not seeing their guide. "Did we turn the wrong way?"

"I don't know," Parker replied, wondering if it had been a figment of her imagination this whole time. But Rider had seen it, too. She wasn't making it up.

"Let's rest for a second. Try to get our bearings."

Parker leaned against one of the hedges and peered up at the sky, as if the moon's position might tell her something even though she knew nothing about astronomy.

"We've got to be close."

But when Parker looked back down, she nearly jumped out of her skin.

The figure was there, standing just three feet away from them. Only, it wasn't moving anymore. It stood stock-still, its arms outstretched as if it wanted to give her a hug, frozen in that uncomfortable pose like a statue. And Parker suddenly realized what it was.

Cautiously, she edged forward. And as she did, the arms turned into twisting branches. The violets on its dress stood out in the pale moonlight. And the figure came into full view.

She'd been so unnerved by this thing the first time she'd stumbled across it. But now, after seeing her own statue's likeness, she felt a kindredness to it. She understood its tragic backstory. That the woman it was meant to represent had been sacrificed.

Parker drew closer, hypnotized, wondering if her statue would find a home in the maze, too. She could see the crown of roses perched on this one's head. She was close enough to touch it if she just reached out her hand.

"Watch out," Rider shouted, and Parker jerked back as something flashed through the night, its metal blades slick and shining and sharp. It snipped through the air and the statue lurched backward, a blur moving in front of Parker, its hand gone, lopped off at the wrist. "You're being awfully naughty tonight," a voice said reproachfully. And Parker scrambled away, pushing herself and Rider to the hedge wall as Sister Florence hobbled out from the shadows, her large garden shears held threateningly in her hands.

"What did you do to Dani?" Parker shrieked, wanting to dive at the woman but afraid to after she'd seen how well she could wield those shears.

"Your friend is with Rosamund," Sister Florence said. "Waiting for you. But we can deal with that next. First, I have to teach someone here a lesson."

The old woman cackled as she opened the shears again and advanced on the statue, forcing it to retreat a few steps. Parker shivered as she realized that the thing really was alive. That it'd been helping her all along.

"Mildred, you know better than to misbehave."

Mildred?

Parker puzzled over that name, not sure how she knew it. And then it hit her.

Mildred Price. The girl from the painting at the headmaster's house. Coronation's first Rose Duchess.

"Don't hurt her," Parker found herself yelling as she rushed forward and lunged at Sister Florence. Rider joined her, and the two of them grappled with the nun. Parker grabbed the shears and tried to wrestle them away from the old woman while Rider grabbed her around the waist and pushed her back.

But Sister Florence wasn't as frail as she looked. She must have had some of Rosamund's power coursing through her. She planted herself in the ground and held on tight. She knocked Parker and Rider off, standing over them, the shears primed to descend in a final guillotine chop. But Mildred was there. She grabbed the woman's wrist with her one remaining hand and continued the fight.

They struggled for a few seconds, and then Sister Florence broke free, delivering a clip to Mildred's torso and then another one to her leg. Mildred faltered as she shed a branch, as a handful of flowers tore loose from her dress. But she stayed on her feet. Stayed in the fight, even though she was losing.

Sister Florence ripped the shears free again and went in for a kill shot, narrowly missing Mildred's neck. She reared back, but right as she was about to plunge her weapon into Mildred's chest, another figure materialized from the shadows. Its feet clomped in the grass as it ran, its music-note earrings tinkling like wind chimes as it moved. And Parker knew before she heard Rider's sharp gasp. She knew that this was Morgan coming to their aid.

There was a crash as the statue rushed past them and collided with Sister Florence, the three figures tussling there in the night. Parker barely managed to scurry out of the way as the garden shears fell to the ground, stabbing themselves in the earth. She watched as Sister Florence sprang back, as the woman leveled her gaze at all of them and pulled out a set of small clippers from underneath her robes.

Mildred's statue stood tall between them, bruised but not broken. It hazarded a glance back at Parker while Morgan's statue bent and helped Rider get to his feet.

The brother and sister met each other's gazes, the words sticking in Rider's mouth. The shock was evident on his face.

He must have expected that he'd never see her again. Especially like this.

But there she was, offering him a hand, pressing her bark-covered palm into his cheek. Parker could see the tears welling up in his eyes. Could see his arms twitching to wrap around her, to pull her into a hug that just might break her fragile body. And as Parker watched them reunite, she wished that it could stretch on forever. She wished that they could make up for everything they had lost in this single moment.

"I'm sorry."

Parker could just make out Rider's whispered words. And she could tell that Morgan had accepted his apology. That she had never blamed him for what had happened to her. It wasn't his fault. His coming out wasn't something he should feel guilty over. They couldn't have known what was going to happen to her. They couldn't have stopped it. But now they could.

Letting go of Rider's hand, Morgan turned and faced Parker, fixing her with that placid stare. Had she been one of Parker's nighttime visitors? She couldn't remember. She'd only ever been able to tell them apart by the colors of their dresses. But they'd been trying to help her all along. She knew that now. They'd meant to warn her, and she hadn't listened. She hadn't understood. But now she did. She wasn't going to let them down anymore.

Together, the statues nodded at Parker, as if they could

read her mind. As if they approved of her plan. And then they turned to face Sister Florence, readying themselves for her attack.

"Come on," Parker said, tugging on Rider's arm, dragging him away from his sister. She hated breaking them up, but she needed his help. She couldn't face Rosamund on her own.

"But what about Morgan?" he sputtered. "I can't leave her."

"She'll be okay. I promise."

And as Sister Florence rushed forward, Parker spun away. She plucked the shears out of the ground and pulled Rider with her, not looking back as Mildred and Morgan moved to intercept Sister Florence. As they held the woman off so that Parker and Rider could escape. She ignored the sounds of their scuffle—the thuds and scratches and snips and rustles. She kept going, turning again and again until the sounds of the fight had faded. Until a woman's strangled voice echoed through the maze, what she hoped was Sister Florence's last cry.

But still, Parker didn't stop. She staggered through the maze, her grip tight around the shears. They were her lifeline. Her last defense. As long as she had them, she wouldn't go down without a fight. She'd take on anyone who stood in her way. Anyone who tried to offer her up as a sacrifice. Anyone who tried to hurt Dani. She wasn't afraid anymore. She didn't have that luxury. It was win or lose. Do or die.

But when Parker stumbled through the last opening in the maze walls, her resolve suddenly wavered. Her knees shook underneath her, and she almost dropped to the ground right there. She knew where she was now. She'd made it here again. Somehow. She was back in the center, only this time, she wasn't alone.

"I'm glad you could join us," the headmaster said, his voice calm as he stood there at the altar in the middle of the clearing, Dani's body lying there at his feet. "I knew you'd make it to us eventually. It was good to have the insurance policy, though. Just in case you decided to run."

And a horrible realization dawned on Parker. Had they planned on sacrificing Dani if Parker hadn't shown up? If she'd decided to run?

"But now that you're here," the headmaster went on, "we can get started."

Torches flickered on either side of him, and Parker could just make out Mrs. York, Brady, and Beth standing there behind him.

"It's been a long wait, but Rosamund is ready for you."

Parker's stomach turned as she spotted the statue standing there beside the headmaster, that familiar figure that she'd danced around only weeks ago. The woman who had haunted her dreams.

Rosamund.

The statue was transforming. The gnarled branches and dried leaves were growing smooth and flexible in the moon-light. Pale skin was stretching across the woman's cheeks.

Blond hair had sprouted from her head, and her fingers were hardening into bone and meat and claws.

The figure shuddered and shook off its vegetative state, discarding the useless layer like a snake shedding its old skin.

And there she was. The demon from Parker's nightmares. Rosamund, in the flesh.

CHAPTER
THIRTY-FOUR

"You're not real," Parker stuttered, her mind unable to process what was right in front of her. "You're just a story. You burned. They killed you."

Rosamund cocked her head as if Parker had told a joke. A smile unfurled on her lips—lips so red against her pale face that it made her look like she'd just taken a bite out of someone.

"I burned," she replied, her mouth opening wide with each word, enunciating every single syllable, "so that I could be resurrected."

A numbness seeped through Parker's body, settling into her bones. She couldn't feel her toes. She couldn't lift her arm. She couldn't turn away from this monster. And next to her, she could feel Rider's body shutting down, too. She could hear his body shivering, his teeth chattering in the night.

"When they ran out of supplies on the ship," Rosamund said, "they fed my rose with their own blood. They kept me alive with the only thing they had to give. With the only thing more precious than water."

She turned to the headmaster and Mrs. York and Brady and Beth, all of whom were looking at her with reverence, their necks bowed ever so slightly to her call.

"Do you know how powerful that is? I couldn't turn away from that devotion. I couldn't abandon my people like that. When winter came and they called out for my help, I answered."

Rosamund's fingers danced in the moonlight, playing along the stem of the Rose of York, the flower that had been blooming here for hundreds of years. The one Coronation's settlers had brought across the Atlantic from their home in England. The rose that had started it all.

"So the stories are real," Parker muttered to herself in disbelief.

"Of course they are." Rosamund's eyes snapped up to find Parker's again.

"And all of you?" Parker looked to the headmaster, afraid of the answer but needing to hear it all the same.

"We've been by Rosamund's side from the beginning. Her most loyal disciples," the headmaster said.

And it all suddenly made sense.

That was why he looked virtually identical to his ancestor

in the paintings at his house. That was why Mrs. York's likeness had been lifting that toast to Mildred Price, the first Rose Duchess. That was why when he spoke about Coronation's first days, he spoke from memory.

He had been there. His whole family had.

Parker took a step back, and suddenly Brady was behind her. He looked terrible, his head bruised and bloody from the whack she'd given him with that shovel. But he was still on his feet. Still intimidating and massive and mean. He towered in front of Parker, ready to grab her, to deliver her to his dad. Rider moved to push him aside, but Brady wasn't playing. He reared back with one fist and socked the boy in the stomach, popping Rider like a balloon, leaving him in a crumpled mass on the ground.

But he didn't leave it at that. He lifted his foot and brought it down on Rider's knee, the sickening *crunch* deafening. Rider writhed in pain, howling, rolling on the ground. He tried to get up, but Brady knocked him down again, his laughter cruel and unlike the boy Parker thought she'd known.

"Stop it," Parker screamed, snapping out of her daze. She swung the shears at Brady, but the boy was faster. He caught her wrists and squeezed, the pain so bad that she couldn't hold on anymore.

The shears slipped from her hand, thudding on the grass, and just like that, she was defenseless. She was trapped. She couldn't save herself or Rider or Dani. Brady pinned her elbow to her side and thrust her forward, leading her toward the altar, toward where Rosamund stood waiting.

"Don't be afraid," Rosamund purred, reaching out to accept Parker's hand. "It's an honor to be chosen. This sacrifice will give your life meaning. You'll live on in me. Your ashes will seed my rebirth."

Suddenly, Parker remembered the fertilizer in Sister Florence's satchel. Whose ashes had she spread that day?

A new terror gripping her, Parker bucked against Brady's hold. She dug her feet into the ground, but he was stronger than her. He had more bulk. She couldn't shake herself loose. She couldn't knock him off balance. She couldn't do anything. And Rider couldn't help her. He was still lying on the ground, doing his best to claw his way toward her.

"Accept your fate," Rosamund said. "There's no use fighting it. Prepare to join all the Rose Duchesses who have come before you."

Rosamund's icy fingers pressed into Parker's wrist. They chilled her pulse. Sent a shiver through her veins. This was it.

Her head dipped and she saw Dani lying there next to the altar. The girl still hadn't moved, which worried Parker. But she could see the rise in her best friend's chest. The small breaths going in and out.

"You can have me," Parker exclaimed, pouring every bit of energy she had left into her voice. "Just promise you'll let her go. She's not part of this. Use your tricks. Make her forget."

Rosamund paused, apparently considering the offer. And for a moment, Parker thought she might even take her up on it. But then the demon cracked her lips into a wicked smile, and she bared her thorny teeth.

"Silly girl. Why would I do a thing like that?"

She opened her mouth then, and her laughter rang out through the center of the maze. And Parker swore she could hear music in her voice. Could hear that chant looping over and over again.

Ring around the Rosie,
A pocket full of posies,
Ashes, ashes,
We all fall down.

Her gaze fell on Dani and tears slid down her cheeks. She had so many regrets. So many things she wished she'd done differently.

"I'm sorry," she whispered, and she let her head drop, surrendering to her fate, letting that music fill her head, sweeping her away like it had on that day at the Bloom Festival. When she'd spun in a circle and joined in their song. When she'd gotten her first taste of Rosamund. When she'd been named Rose Duchess and set this whole thing in motion.

"What are you doing here?"

The headmaster's voice echoed through the clearing,

cutting through the daze that had overcome Parker, snapping her awake. She craned her neck around and saw a group of shadows converging at the opening to the maze.

"Sister Florence?" the headmaster called, irritation lacing his words. "Your pets need tending to."

But no one answered. Sister Florence certainly couldn't. Mildred and Morgan had already taken care of her.

"Begone."

The headmaster waved an aggravated hand at them, but the figures didn't move. They loomed in the entrance, as menacing as ever. But not to Parker. Not anymore. She knew who they were. She knew that they were her sisters.

"I said—" the headmaster blustered, but he didn't get to finish.

As if Mildred had flashed a signal, the figures attacked, darting through the night, intercepting Mrs. York and Beth, jerking Brady off Parker's back, causing her to stumble out of Rosamund's grasp.

"The girl," Rosamund yelled as she pointed in Parker's direction.

But she didn't come after Parker herself. She stayed put, knocking the Rose Duchesses away as they threw themselves at her, protecting the Rose of York with its milky-white petals.

And in that chaos, Parker thought she heard someone calling her name. She turned and saw Rider gesturing wildly at her, playing some sort of elaborate game of charades. She didn't know what he was trying to tell her, but then she saw his arm winding back. She saw a glimmer in the night as he tossed something in her direction. She reached out to catch it, but her fingers were sweaty and shaking. She fumbled it and it fell to the ground, the glass shattering on impact. She scurried to pick up the pieces, and her heart jumped into her throat as a cloud of metallic-green beetles rose into the air, Rider's pets taking flight, making straight for Rosamund and the Rose of York she was protecting. But they wouldn't be enough to create the swarm Rider had hoped.

Parker realized what she had to do.

Scrambling back, she kept low to the ground as she scanned the grass, searching frantically. They had to be here somewhere.

"Over there." Rider grimaced, using all the strength he had left to lift his arm. And Parker spotted it, too. She pounced, her fingers closing around the wooden handles, lifting the garden shears from where they'd fallen when Brady had grabbed her.

Whipping around, Parker narrowed her eyes at Rosamund. The demon wasn't paying attention to her. She had her hands full with the Rose Duchesses. And Beth and Brady were similarly occupied, fighting their own battles. This was Parker's chance. Sprinting forward, she raised the shears in front of her, the blades open, ready to slice. Ready to cut. Ready to sever.

"Not so fast," the headmaster shouted as he threw his body in Parker's way.

But she had expected the move. She'd seen him coming. Ducking underneath him, she brought her arms around, swinging the flat side of the garden shears into his shins, knocking him clean off his feet as she let her momentum propel her forward.

He fell with a garbled scream, but Parker didn't waste any time watching. She shot forward, her goal in sight. She opened the shears, ready to deliver the blow. And as the blades pinched around the rose's stem, Parker found that it cut easily. She barely had to put any pressure on it and the metal slid shut.

"No!" the headmaster wailed, lunging for Parker.

But it was too late. The Rose of York was already falling, plummeting to the ground, its stalk severed at the base. And Rosamund was following suit. She pitched forward, her body rigid, crashing to the ground in one sweeping motion, a felled tree surrendering to gravity.

The headmaster rushed over and grabbed Rosamund, cradling her broken body in his lap. Tears slid down his cheeks as he prayed over her. As he grieved.

"You," he snarled, and he turned back toward Parker. He glared at her with rage-filled eyes. "You ruined everything."

And he jumped to his feet, trying to tackle Parker, lunging right for her neck.

She danced out of his way and he knocked into the altar

instead. He jostled the torches and one fell from its holder. It rolled off the table and into the grass, its flames catching on Rosamund's body, starting to smoke.

Like hay in late summer, her gown ignited. The flames burned hot and fast. They consumed her, her pale skin flaking, disintegrating into ashes in seconds.

Parker whirled around as the headmaster roared in pain. She spotted him writhing on the ground, his whole body convulsing uncontrollably. And then she saw Brady and Mrs. York and Beth all doing the same. Their screams filled the clearing as invisible flames licked over their limbs, as their flesh withered, drying out to a husk, turning to dust that sank into the earth and scattered away on the wind.

And then there was silence.

Parker let it roll over her, afraid of what would happen if she moved. Afraid that the nightmare wouldn't be over.

But it was. It had to be. Rosamund was gone. The Yorks had crumbled to dust. Her curse was broken. They were safe.

Somewhere inside Parker, a dam cracked and she fell to her knees. Her hands dug into the grass and she started to cry, relief spilling over her.

She heard someone coughing and looked up to see Dani stirring. She jumped to her feet and rushed to her friend's side, wanting to be the first thing she saw when she woke up.

"Is that you?" Dani croaked, her eyes still half-closed.

"You're alive," Parker exclaimed, pulling the girl into a hug, not caring if she squeezed too tightly. She'd lost Dani once and she never wanted to let her go again.

"And you're crying," Dani replied, sitting up slowly, holding her head like the world was swimming around her. "What happened?"

"It's a long story," Parker said. "And I promise that I'll explain later. But first—"

Here, Parker faltered. But she pushed through anyway, knowing she had to get the words out. Knowing she couldn't wait a single second longer.

"First I wanted to say that I'm sorry. For everything. I should have listened to you. I shouldn't have pressured you into doing that stupid prank. I shouldn't have left you there to take the fall. I should have stuck by your side. I should have—"

There was so much she wanted to apologize for. Too much, actually. So she tried to keep it simple and hoped it would be enough.

"I missed you." Parker held her breath as she waited, only letting it out when Dani smiled, repeating those same words back to her.

"I missed you, too."

And they pulled each other into another hug, tears spilling down both of their faces now.

"Are you good to walk?" Parker asked. And Dani nodded slowly, only stumbling once as she got to her feet, Parker moving in to catch her, to offer a shoulder for her to lean on.

Carefully, they picked their way across the clearing, heading to where Rider was sitting up, his knee swollen to twice its normal size. A smile played on his lips, making him look happy even though he was clearly in pain.

"You did it." He grimaced.

"All thanks to you," Parker said. "And them."

She gestured to the Rose Duchesses assembled around them, the statues that had come to their rescue.

Dani's mouth fell open.

"I promise, I'll explain everything," Parker said.

They were helping each other up now, examining where they'd lost limbs, snapping branches back into place. Then, after dusting themselves off, they crept back into the maze, a parade of lilies and violets and daffodils floating by until there were only two of them left. Mildred and Morgan. The first and the last.

They came closer and stood next to Parker, Rider, and Dani. They looked at them with those open eyes and wordless mouths. Then Morgan bent over and picked up her brother. She cradled him in her arms, pressing a kiss to his forehead, sharing an unspoken thought with him.

"Thank you," he whispered as Morgan pulled away. "For saving us. And for forgiving me." Mildred started walking, Morgan following in her wake, carrying Rider in her arms. Parker and Dani fell in line behind them and they moved through the maze in silence, Parker too weary to marvel at what she would have believed impossible only a few hours before. They turned corners, passed down narrow corridors, and before she knew it, they were back at the maze entrance.

The gardens opened up in front of them, but there was something different in the air. Parker inhaled, and she realized that the scent of roses was gone. She walked to a nearby bush and touched where the flowers had withered, where they'd turned to ash just like Rosamund.

In the distance she could hear groans. She could see the light of the bonfire and shadows stumbling away from it. A man passed within sight, muttering to himself, clearly confused, rubbing his eyes like he'd just woken from a long nightmare. And Parker knew that Rosamund's spell was truly broken.

She turned back to the maze, to Mildred and Morgan, but the Rose Duchesses had disappeared. Only Rider and Dani were there, sitting peacefully on the grass. She smiled at them and padded over. The two girls lifted his weight on their shoulders, and together, they started the trek across the gardens, taking their time, knowing that they didn't have any more monsters on their heels.

CHAPTER
THIRTY-FIVE

"Is that everything?" Parker's dad hollered from the driveway as he stuffed a duffel bag into the back of the car.

"There are a few more boxes in the kitchen," Parker's mom replied as she shouldered open the front door and came out with her arms full. She set it all on the porch and wiped her forehead. She looked back at the house and shook her head.

"I can't believe it's only been a month," she marveled. "Are you sure you're okay with moving again? I know we said we'd stay for a while."

"It's fine," Parker said, getting up from the porch steps. "We're city people. It's where we belong."

Parker's mom smiled at her and then got back to packing, carrying the boxes out to the car while Parker watched. With the Yorks gone and the Rosarium out of business, her dad was back on the hunt for a new job. Luckily, he'd already lined up a few leads in DC, so they were heading home.

As Parker watched her parents pack, she looked for signs of change. She hadn't noticed much of a shift in their behavior since the bonfire. It was subtle, if anything. Not like some of the people who had lived in Coronation for years. They were still shaking off the effects of Rosamund's control. Spacing out in the aisles at the grocery store. Waking up in the middle of Main Street having sleepwalked a mile to get there. Forgetting places and people and names, their memories hazy, as if they'd been trapped in a dream for their entire lives.

"One last trip and I think we'll be ready," Parker's dad said, ruffling Parker's hair as he passed and disappeared into the house, Parker's mom following right behind him, leaving Parker alone. But not for long.

"I can't believe you're already going." Rider stood at the end of the driveway, leaning on a pair of crutches, his knee wrapped in an inch of bandages. Parker leapt off the porch and jogged down to meet him.

"How did you get out here?"

"My mom."

Rider gestured at the driveway, to where a woman was waiting in the car, her nails gleaming a metallic green on top of the steering wheel.

"She let me paint them last night," Rider explained as he held up his own hands for Parker to see. "Matching sets."

"And how are they doing with everything?"

"Not great." Rider shrugged. "But better. They still think Morgan died in an accident. But at least they're grieving now, which they didn't get to do before. Not really. It's a step in the right direction."

"Are you going to tell them what actually happened?" Parker asked.

"No. It's too much. They'd blame themselves. If they even believed me."

Parker understood that. Her parents had no idea what had gone on in that hedge maze. And she wanted to keep it that way. Either they'd think she was making it all up, or they'd be so worried that they'd never let her leave the house again.

"So are you all staying?" Parker asked.

"For now."

But Parker could hear the hope in his voice. And she suspected that he had a trip to the gardens planned as soon as he was back on both his feet. A visit to see if he could find Morgan again.

"I'm sad you're leaving, though. I'm going to miss you."

"Even after everything I put you through?" Parker asked. "If I'd just believed you from the start, I could have saved us all this trouble."

"But then we wouldn't have stopped Rosamund. And you wouldn't have made up with Dani. And I wouldn't have found Morgan."

He grew serious all of a sudden, so Parker wrapped her arms around his shoulders and gave him her biggest hug. She was happy that he'd found closure. Happy that he didn't hold on to that guilt anymore.

"So how are things with Dani?" he asked, pulling away, no doubt changing the subject so he wouldn't cry all over her.

"They're better," Parker said. "She's already back in DC. She's in major trouble with her parents for coming up here without telling them. But I think she'll survive. I put in a good word. Told her mom that I had begged her to come visit. I still can't believe you convinced her to take a ten-hour bus just to check in on me."

It amazed Parker. Dani had traveled this far just because a stranger had told her that she was in trouble.

"I didn't have to do any convincing," Rider insisted. "I just asked her to give you a call. I thought she could get through to you. She got the idea for that bus all by herself."

And she had. Parker knew that now. She and Dani had talked about it. Dani had wanted to patch things up all along. It was Parker who hadn't been willing to reach out. She'd been so worried and embarrassed and guilt-ridden about what she'd done that she hadn't thought Dani could ever forgive her. So she hadn't given her the chance.

"I owe you one," Parker said, a smile flitting across her face.

"At this point, I think we're even."

And maybe they were.

As Parker stood there in the driveway, her last moments in Coronation ticking away, she sucked in a deep breath. She let it fill her nose and mouth and lungs. She held on to it, the pressure in her chest building, a balloon ready to burst. And then she blew it out in one long stream, relieved that it wasn't sweet. That she didn't smell a single hint of rose in the air.

ACKNOWLEDGMENTS

I have so many people to thank for their help in creating *A Pocket Full of Posies*. Without them this book simply would not exist.

Thank you to my editor, Samantha Palazzi, for her insightful notes and patience as I worked through the first draft. The process of writing this book was hard, and it wouldn't have gotten to where it is without Sam's help. I'd also like to thank everyone working behind-the-scenes. Tony Mauro created an amazing cover. Thank you to the book designer, Chris Stengel, and the production editor, Janell Harris. Also thank you to the copy editor Jessica White and the proofreaders Peter Kranitz, Susan Hom, and Cindy Durand. Thanks to the Fairs and Clubs managers Janna Haussman and Kristin Standley for getting behind this book. I still can't believe that it's going to be in schools across the country. Thanks especially to my amazing publicist, Daniela Escobar, for all the shouting she's done about my books. Also thanks to the entire sales team at Scholastic. Working in sales myself, I'll always have a soft spot for the hard work you do in getting books into stores in the first place.

Outside of the publishing team, I'd like to thank my family and friends. My parents and brother and Kyle and all my pets. They kept me sane throughout the past year of writing. Thanks to my critique partner, Robby Weber. He read *A Pocket Full of Posies* from the beginning and helped me immensely with his feedback and friendship. (He's also an amazing author himself. If you haven't checked out his debut novel, *If You Change Your Mind*, go and do it now!) Also a big thank-you to my agent, Brent Taylor, and everyone else at Triada US.

And lastly, thank you to all the readers out there. Without your support, I wouldn't get to keep writing.

ABOUT THE AUTHOR

Shawn Sarles was born and raised in a small town in western Kentucky. *A Pocket Full of Posies* is his third book. He currently lives in the Philadelphia area and continues to write horror for teens.